BARBARA BLEIMAN

Kremlinology of Kisses

Blue Door Press

First published in 2020
By Blue Door Press
London, UK
https://bluedoorpress.co.uk

Typeset in Baskerville/Avenir

A CIP record for this book is available from the British Library

ISBN: 978-1-9164754-3-4

By the same author

FICTION

Off the Voortrekker Road

Accidents of Love

EDUCATION

What Matters in English Teaching

Praise for *Kremlinology of Kisses*

Barbara Bleiman's *Kremlinology of Kisses* is an absorbing, entertaining and often moving short-story collection. Each story instantly and intimately involves the reader and makes you want to read on to the end to find out what happens. Bleiman's precise, economical prose vividly evokes a remarkable variety of characters, situations, emotions, times and places. The recurrent motif of the kiss grows in significance throughout the book, creating a bond between the individual stories that helps to make the collection a rich and multi-faceted whole.

Nicolas Tredell, Consultant Editor, Palgrave Macmillan Essential Criticism Guides

Barbara Bleiman's stories range across time and continents, but always return to women's lives and the penetrating questions of love. I thoroughly enjoyed being immersed in these rich slices of life.

Kate Clanchy, winner of
The Orwell Prize for Political Writing 2020

'Though it seems to me like the wildest of dreams, beyond the range of possibility, it is really a very commonplace thing,' Riabovitch mused [...] 'It is very usual and happens to everyone... '

Anton Chekhov, 'The Kiss'

Contents

Kremlinology of Kisses

'Three, Gregor,' his wife told him, as they stood at the door of the apartment. 'It must be three kisses.' She was brushing his winter coat with the beaver-hair clothes brush she kept on the stand in the hall. His shoes were polished to a mirror-like shine and his overboots too had been scraped clean of the mud and street mire that invariably clung to them once the snow had melted and dried. On top of the large wood burner, his old fur hat was warming nicely. The evening before, she had trimmed his hair, tidied his moustache, clipped the hairs in his nostrils and his ears. She had pinned his medal to the lapel of his jacket. Bestowed on him in 1975 for Distinguished Labour it had lain unused for the past few months, but now it seemed important to bring it back into service. That morning she had made him pancakes with loganberry sauce for his breakfast, his favourite, with coffee brewed from water she'd heated earlier in the samovar. The coffee had been of a good quality – not the usual rubbish she had to make do with, adulterated with chicory or perhaps even sawdust.

She'd bought a little packet of beans especially, from a woman she could trust. Black market. She had taken pleasure in grinding them herself, knowing that he would have the very best, this morning.

'Take care of yourself,' he said, before he left. He patted her stomach. 'All will be well, my love. I promise.' At last, after all those years of wanting and waiting, when they had given up entirely, she had amazed them both by fainting at work one day and discovering that she was well on the way to having a baby. She had worked through till her eighth month and here she was, on maternity leave, putting her feet up for the first time in her life. But now there was so much time to think, so much time to worry.

When he left she returned to the kitchen and sat down for a moment at the table. A little coffee remained in the pot, so she poured the dregs into a cup, added some sugar, put it on the stove to warm again and then drank it slowly, savouring the rich, strong taste. He had gone now. There was nothing more she could do, only wait. But the hours stretched out like a long road that would never come to an end. She thought of the years she'd spent in the village with her mother, walking, walking, walking along the road to the school in the nearest town, with nothing but the flat fields and her own thoughts to occupy her. Now her day lay ahead, with countless seconds and minutes and many hours till he would be back, till she would know what their fate would be.

It had been a hard life, before she met him. Her mother was a simple woman, and not well connected. Though she herself was clever and determined, and had gained excellent marks in school, she had had no illusions that success would just fall into her lap and, as expected, it had not proved easy to climb the ladder. Marrying Gregor had been a stroke of good fortune. He was a middle-rank official in the Party organisation in the next town, a growing centre of mining and industry. She had been given work there as a lowly administrative assistant and only observed him from afar in the corridors, never coming to his attention as he strode past her. But then one day, when winter flu swept across the steppes and struck the whole division, with many of her colleagues forced to take to their beds, she found herself in his office, taking notes at a meeting that should have been attended by the superior of her superior's superior. He noticed her and, despite the fact that he was said to have been courting her superior's superior's daughter, he made it known that she was of some interest to him.

Soon it became clear that she was of more than some interest to him. He asked for her specifically at meetings, required her to accompany him on visits to a mine or a factory, even invited her to the annual Party awards ceremony for local officials whose work had made a major contribution to the achievement of their targets. Because she was a clever young woman, she understood that she had to play her hand carefully. She was not one of those silly girls who succumbed too quickly to flattery and a whiff of power, who were just out for an extra luxury or two, a silk scarf, a good meal of freshly slaughtered meat and some decent vodka. She accepted his invitations, his gifts and his attentions but kept a careful distance, always catching the last bus back to her mother's house rather than being tempted to stay in town.

The day he proposed to her was the best day of her life. She felt a heavy weight had been lifted from her. She could breathe at last. No longer would she have to struggle to pay the rent for her mother's house in the village and count the coins to make sure there was enough left for fuel and food. No longer would she worry about repairs to the roof or the cost of new shoes for the winter or the looming possibility that her mother might fall ill and need additional support.

It took a while to adjust to her new life and her new home in the apartment he was able to provide right in the centre of the town. But adjust she did. And soon, she became accustomed to the little extras that came with being the wife of a middle-rank official in the Party. She enjoyed being greeted on the street with a polite nod of respect from the women she passed, the security of knowing that when the queues for food were long and the shelves bare, Gregor would always be able to bring home some of what she required for their daily needs. She took pleasure in the opportunities it gave to show pity for some lesser person of her acquaintance, demonstrating her generosity by giving them a little gift of food or a small item that would signal her greater prosperity. Being the wife of Gregor had changed her life for the better.

As she grew more comfortable as the wife of Gregor Popov, the mid-ranking but steadily rising official of the Party in the town of Stalinsk, she forgot the suffering of her childhood and the years before. She put it behind her, as if it had never been, as if she had always been Paulina Popova, wife of Gregor. Her mother was now living in the apartment with them, so she had no need to visit the old house, or the village, and be reminded of her humble beginnings. It was as if that earlier life belonged to a different person, a girl who happened to share her name but had little else in common with the person she had become.

Now though, as she sat at the kitchen table, she thought again of those times. She remembered the hardship and the bleak sense of one day following another, in an unending, muddy river that flowed on and on, sluggish and monotonous, with no change and no prospect of change. She tried to shut out these unwelcome thoughts but it was hard to do so, on this day. For weeks she had succeeded well enough. She had forced herself to think with hope. She had said to herself that Gregor was highly respected. He had climbed high. His rise had been faster than most. He had the ear of his superior, and his superior's superior. They wished to see him succeed. He was sharp-witted, alert, able to sniff out signs of trouble that might go unnoticed by others. He knew how to talk to people, how to smooth things over, how to be of most assistance, how to oil the wheels. He never spoke amiss, always careful to say just as much as was needed and no more. He waited till his superior, or his superior's superior, had spoken, and then and only then did he venture an opinion of his own, following closely the line of thought he had heard, often even using their very words, offering them back as a form of compliment, avoiding any risk of introducing a dangerous nuance of his own.

He told her all this, when he came home each evening, after taking off his coat, his hat, his overshoes, his shoes, putting on his warm slippers and coming to sit in the chair by the stove. He went through each detail, of how he had managed his affairs in the office that day and how it had been received, confirming with himself that he had judged aright, that he had said the right thing, made the right gesture, nodded in agreement at the right time. 'You were absolutely correct to say that, do that, behave in that way,' she always said, stroking his hand and reassuring him, though she had little idea of the circumstances beyond what he told her. 'You are so good at these things,' she said.

And then, just a week ago, he had come home and told her that that day, straight after his lunch, he had received a visit from his superior, telling him that his superior's superior wished to see him. He had heard from his superior, who had heard from someone of his own rank, who had heard from someone of a rank beneath him, that he had been heard talking about the target for the year in the factory in the town. Apparently, he had been expressing concern that it might not be met. He had been offering reasons why and ways in which this might be resolved. His superior told him that his superior's superior appreciated his concern and wished to talk to him, along with the Head of the Division. They were interested to know his views.

He came home in a state of shock. How was he to read this? His superior had been friendly. He had smiled when he told him. He had shaken his hand. Gregor had looked at her sheepishly. He *had* been talking about the targets, he said, but not wildly, not openly. He had mentioned his concerns to Vasily Vasiliev, his dear friend Vasily, who, though on a level with his superior, was not someone to talk to him about matters other than those directly involved with their own work. He would never talk to him about Gregor and their private conversations. Never. Not unless, of course, Vasily thought that this might do Gregor some good. Perhaps Vasily had talked of Gregor's important ideas, his constructive suggestions to help them meet the targets and be of assistance to everyone in the division. That must be it, Gregor thought. Vasily had done him an immense favour. If his ideas were liked, he would be promoted. Though one could never be sure. He did not like to step off the track into the unknown, unless sure of where he was going. He was always careful. Very, very careful. But now he seemed to have, indeed, stepped off and was heading into tall grasses and marshland and thick undergrowth, not knowing quite where to place his foot next.

She sat at the table and sighed. It had been a trying week. Gregor had not been sleeping well. His appetite was poor. She was glad she had made him the pancakes and, now that the day of the meeting was here, he had eaten them, seemingly with relish. He had an air of confidence when he left, a look of optimism. It was important to appear strong, not to seem nervous or timid. Timidity suggested that you had something to hide, she thought. Gregor looked, instead, as if he had something important to say, something useful to offer. She reassured herself with that thought.

As the day wore on though, she found herself feeling increasingly anxious. She felt the baby kick and instead of responding with a surge of joy, she frowned. What kind of life was this baby coming into? She busied herself tidying the apartment, attending to her mother's needs and making something especially tasty for their evening meal, beetroot soup with sour cream and a hearty cabbage stuffed with minced lamb. But still the feelings of unease crept in. In just a few hours' time, they might be celebrating Gregor's promotion to a new, important role, or... She wouldn't even allow herself to think about the alternative. It was too awful.

When he walked through the door, she would ask him. Did your superior's superior kiss you twice on the cheeks? Or was it three times? Then she would know. Once spelt disaster; she couldn't contemplate that. Twice was not good. Three times was what she hoped for. A firm grasp on the shoulders, a smile and then three kisses, planted firmly. Of course, there were other possibilities. But three kisses were what was needed, for them to feel secure. They would know that whatever had been said could be trusted; it was meant. That would be good news.

She remembered Gregor telling her about watching, on the small television screen given to the Head of the Division, the greeting between their great leader, Brezhnev, and the leader of the GDR, Erich Honecker, the day of the 30th anniversary of the Republic. They had gathered in his office to watch it as it happened. A bottle of vodka was on hand to toast the historic occasion. There had been smiles all round as the great leader reached towards Comrade Honecker and kissed him heartily three times. They had all witnessed the cementing of a relationship that would never fail or fade. The Soviet Union and the GDR, Brezhnev and Honecker, a marriage of leaders and countries that would last for ever. The kisses sealed it. For ever.

From the next room, she heard her mother noisily clearing her throat. She must have woken from her afternoon sleep. Paulina waited for the sound of the squeaking bed springs as her mother reached for her stick to bang hard on the wooden floor, the familiar signal that her help was needed. When the thumping started, Paulina raised herself carefully from her chair. Her legs were swollen and her stomach heavy; she lumbered across the kitchen towards the door, squeezing herself awkwardly between the table and the dresser.

'I'm coming, Mama,' she called.

On the way, she stopped at the lavatory to collect the chamber pot.

'Be quick. I'm bursting,' her mother shouted.

She sighed. When the baby came there would be yet another life to sustain and nurture. Her mother and Gregor took up every ounce of her energy already; she wondered how she would find the time and space for another being.

'I'm coming, Mama,' she called again. She must hurry now, or her mother would not be able to wait, and then there would be even more work, stripping the bed and washing the sheets.

But fortunately, she was in time and, when her mother was done, she helped her into the chair by the bed and covered her knees with the old camel-wool blanket. She found her felt slippers and knelt down to ease them onto her feet.

Her mother patted her head gently. 'You're a good girl, a good daughter,' she said. 'You've done well for yourself and for me.'

Paulina heaved herself up from the ground, using the bedstead as a support. She kissed her mother on the top of her head. She was glad that she'd been able to bring Mama to live with them when she'd married Gregor. All being well, Mama would spend her remaining days in comfort. Not everyone could do that for their parent. All being well, Mama would live to see the first years of her grandchild's life; she would get to play the role of babushka; she would die happy. All being well.

And now, at last, it was the time for Gregor's return. He was always punctual. He arrived no earlier than six p.m., no later than five minutes past. And here she was at seven minutes past, still waiting, looking out of the window down at the street, watching for him. A sense of panic flooded through her. What if he wasn't coming back? What if they had taken him away? She might never see him again. She, and her child, might be forced back into that other life, the one she had so happily left behind.

And now, it was ten minutes past, and she heard footsteps on the echoing stairs and rustling sounds on the landing outside the door, and he was here. Thank God, she thought. At least he is home.

'How many?' she asked. 'How many kisses?'

'None,' he said, and she felt her legs give way. Her head spun and she found herself falling towards the floor. But he reached to catch her and as he held her close to him, he laughed.

'None on the cheeks,' he said, 'but a giant one right smack bang on the lips.' He pressed her closer to him. 'I have a promotion,' he said. 'From now on I will be the superior to my superior.'

She hugged him, holding him tight, and they felt a sudden lurch as the baby moved inside her. He was celebrating with them. 'A promotion,' she said, laughing, 'for my clever husband.'

And then she gave him a kiss too, a giant one right smack bang on the lips.

'There's borscht on the stove, and a great big cabbage stuffed with mince in the oven,' she said at last, when they finally drew apart. 'And tomorrow, I will go out and buy more coffee beans so that you can have proper coffee every single day.'

For ever, she thought of saying, but didn't. She knew better than that.

The Sitting

The Contessa Isabella Flavia Luisa di Lampedusa adjusted the clasp of the diamond that hung from her left ear like a tiny droplet of tears. She smoothed the rustling damask of her full wine-red skirt. She powdered the skin on her neck and in the curve of breasts that were pushed up tight by the bone corsetry of her bodice. She tidied the loose blue-black hairs that had escaped the golden fretwork of her net. She perched carefully on the satinwood chair, with its arms and legs that scrolled down to meet four elaborately carved lion's paws, claws sharp as needles.

The chair sat by a table, next to the window. The Contessa looked out of the window, towards the olive groves and the hills beyond Montalcino, cast in afternoon shadow and the pale flare of a late-September sun. She heard the faraway tolling of the bells in the campanile and in the many other towers on the far side of the valley.

'Entra,' she said, raising her voice to be heard through the heavy oak door.

It opened instantly and the serving woman, Julia Maria, entered, ushering in the young man behind her. 'The painter,' she said. 'To paint your portrait. As usual.'

'I know. Every day when the bells toll for evening prayers. Now go.'

'The Count has told me that I must stay.'

The Contessa flashed a look at her but said nothing.

'Where shall I sit, madam?'

The chamber was richly furnished. There was a walnut cabinet, inlaid with ivory, ebony and bone, and a fine Savonarola chair. A tapestry hung from the stuccoed walls. It showed a man on horseback, skewering a wild boar. The Countess let her eyes sweep across the room, away from the pale light that filtered in through the window, towards its darker recesses.

'Take your sewing into the corner. You can see me well enough from every angle there. You can tell the Count, your master, what looks have passed between me and the painter, whether I stayed seated or stood up to gaze out of the window, when precisely I sighed, or took my embroidered handkerchief to wipe the perspiration from my lip, whether we talked of chiaroscuro or scarlet pigments ground from cochineal, or the cherry trees in the garden below. The corner will be adequate for all of that.'

'Yes, madam. As you wish.'

The painter waited by the door till the exchange was over, then came towards her and took out his box of paints. The easel stood covered but ready, in the middle of the room. He took off his outer garment, a dun-coloured cloak. The Contessa remembered it from his previous visits. She had thought then, as now, that it was thin and ugly, barely serviceable even for the balmy evenings of spring. Beneath the cloak, his shirt was stained with paint and grease, rumpled, perhaps from having been slept in, limp from lack of starch and steam. His grey hose was badly patched and his leather boots unpolished. And yet.

The painter did not look at her. He opened the wooden box he'd brought with him and took out the pigs' bladders filled with the oily paints he had prepared in his studio, pungent-smelling pastes of ground glass and pigment, oglio cotto and beeswax. He was silent as he worked, squeezing the paints onto his palette. The Contessa sat still, her pale hands locked together in her lap. She looked at the colours as they appeared, slipping so easily out of their flabby casings. The yellow of the lemon groves stretching out behind the monastery. The green of winter grass plumped up with rain. The strident purples of medaglie del Papa flowers in the woods of cypress trees and pines in spring. The violent red of the blood hurrying in her veins.

The painter wiped his hands on his tunic. He raised the sheet from the easel and let it drop to the floor. Julia Maria set down her embroidery. She hurried over to pick it up and fold it neatly. She placed it carefully on the stool beside him. The Contessa saw the look of undisguised displeasure that she gave to the painter, before returning to her seat in the corner.

And now the painter was ready. He lowered his head and breathed in deeply. He took up the palette and selected a thin brush from the canvas sleeve he had unrolled. He wiped one hand across his face and swept back the long dark hair that hung over his brow. And then he looked at her.

His eyes travelled up from her soft leather shoe, peeping out from beneath her skirts. They went up towards her hands poised in a firm clasp in her lap, to her narrow waist, held by a tight band of silk, to her breasts, powdered with fine white dust, her slender neck and her slightly angled chin. His eyes moved beyond, to the mole on her cheek and to her eyes, where they rested for a moment. She caught his gaze with her own and held it, saw the strange blueness that blazed out of the olive darkness of his skin, searched it for a moment and then looked down.

He brought the brush up to his face and held it perpendicular before him, as if to measure the distance between forehead and eyebrows, eyes and nose, nose and lips, lips and chin. But his eyes never left her own.

'Julia Maria. Will you fetch me a drink of water from the kitchens?'

'There is a jug on the table, Contessa. I will pour you a glass.'

'It is warm and stale. The water in the kitchens is cool and fresh. I am weary from the heat.'

'I will call to the kitchen maid.'

'You will waken my son from his afternoon sleep.'

'He is sleeping far away, under the trees in the orchard, with the wet nurse watching over him.'

Julia Maria opened the heavy oak door. She shouted down the corridor, so that her voice rang out against the cold stone walls.

'Anna Luisa! Bring fresh water for the Contessa. Straightaway!'

There was the click of a latch and the slow whine of a door creaking open in the room across the corridor. The

Contessa felt the subtle change in the light and a draught of cool air unsettling the still, sleepy heat. She felt eyes resting on the back of her neck, surveying her, looking at the painter, the room. And then she heard the metallic snick, as the door was quietly closed again.

When the fresh jug of water appeared, she allowed the girl to pour her a glass and set it down on the table beside her, then flicked her fingers to tell her to go. She folded her hands in her lap again.

'Your water, madam?' said Julia Maria.

'I am no longer thirsty,' she said.

The painter spoke for the first time.

'Madam, shall we start?'

She sat forward in her seat, stretched her neck and adjusted her gaze, so her eyes followed a line through the window and out to the wooded hills.

'A little more to the left,' he said.

She turned her head slightly.

'Your chin needs to be angled more this way.'

She tilted her head.

'May I?' the painter said. He moved towards her.

Julia Maria's needle went still, its fine silk held unmoving above the cloth.

The painter placed himself carefully next to the Contessa. She sat motionless, looking out of the window. He reached towards her face, with one hand. With two fingers, like a conductor invoking the most perfect pianissimo from his violins, the painter touched her face and turned her chin towards him.

Julia Maria leaned forward in her seat.

The painter edged backwards. He looked at the Contessa.

'Just right,' he said.

He took up his palette and started to paint.

The Contessa sat listening to the brush strokes, the fine scratching of badger hair on canvas. She heard the jangling bells of the goats in the village and the call of the goatherd. She caught the sound of water being sluiced from a bucket into a drain and the shout of Anna Luisa, asking where in the name of Jesu was the man with the partridges that she needed to prepare for the Count's dinner. Finally, she heard the soft, bubbling snore of Julia Maria, whose head had dropped forward and whose needle had slipped from the thread and fallen unnoticed to the floor.

The Contessa turned to look at the painter. It was his ugliness and his beauty that struck her. His nose was too big. It jutted out of his face. It took up too much space. His forehead was low and broad and his eyebrows dark and heavy. His face was rough and unshaven. He looked uncouth, uncomfortable in his skin, more of a farmhand or gardener than a painter. And yet those eyes. Bluebells in the woods or lapis lazuli? Sapphires or diamonds or shallow pools, or the sky on days when the sun sears the skin? No, none of those.

He lifted his eyes from the canvas and looked at her, then back to Julia Maria, slumped forwards in her chair. Slowly, he edged out and away from the easel. Stepping softly in his leather shoes, he moved towards the Contessa. He reached into a pocket of his tunic and brought out a small slip of thin, folded parchment. He opened the Contessa's clasped hand, peeling back her slender fingers one by one.

She could hear his breath coming louder, faster. Carefully, he placed the parchment on her open palm and closed it again. Then, watching her all the while, he stepped back to his canvas and resumed his painting.

There was a sudden start. Julia Maria looked up. She reached down for the needle that had fallen to the floor, then glanced around her. The painter was at his easel and the Contessa was gazing out at the hills, her hands clasped simply in her lap.

The bells rang in the campanile in the village and the Contessa finally turned towards Julia Maria.

'Enough. I am tired. The painter can come again.'

She stood and gently brushed out the creases in her damask skirt. 'Tomorrow, as usual,' she said. And then she moved to go. Julia Maria hurried to open the door for her.

'Let the painter pack away his tools, then see him out,' she said.

She nodded her head towards him and he bowed down low, raising his eyes to look at her only at the very last moment. 'They are like cornflowers,' she thought.

The Contessa went straight to her room and closed the door behind her. She stood resting her back against the oak panels, so that the full length of her body was supported by the hard wood. She closed her eyes.

If there were a key in the lock on her door, she would turn it. If there were a ladder, she would descend it. If there were a marvellous machine that could fly, she would board it and let it carry her, out over the olive and lemon groves, the orchards and fields, the woods, the campanile and the village and away. She would return to her family. She would forgo the partridges and the pheasants. She would rip off the silk and damask and say goodbye to the diamonds and the pearls.

But the painter. The cornflower eyes. And the ugly nose.

She waited till the blood had slowed a little, then opened her palm. Inside, the tiny piece of parchment lay folded, a little damp now from the warmth of her hand. Should she open it? Or would it be safer to just bury it in among the twigs and logs at the hearth, to catch into flames when Anna Luisa came soon to light the fire? If it remained unseen by her, she would never know what the painter had given her. If it remained unseen, she could give nothing away.

She opened it.

It took her a moment to understand what it was. She had expected words, a declaration of devotion, a desperate plea to meet, at this time and at this place, with the help of this or that trusted friend.

Instead it was a drawing. A simple sketch. Two faces, his and hers. His large nose turned to one side. Hers tipped forwards. An awkward angling of features, finding a complicated accommodation. The painter and her, lips touching, eyes open, looking at each other. A kiss.

She took the piece of parchment. She went towards the fire. Then she turned and, folding the paper, she reached down into her bodice, found a space between the hard bone of her corset and the soft linen of her blouse and placed it there. Not safe, but secret, and close enough, for now, to the beating of her heart.

Isidore

It was a hot day for a funeral. The cooling winds of the 'Cape Doctor' had stilled and, in the apartment that Mama and I lived in above Krapotkin's the butcher's, the air hung heavy and stale. I sat on the old floral sofa trying to read my *Action Comics* book and ignore her preparations. She had been standing on the piano stool, trying to reach a box on top of the armoire. Now she stepped down and pushed the stool to one side.

'Come here, Benjamin. Let me lift you up. See if *you* can reach that stubborn bloody box. It's over to the left there, right at the back.'

She raised me up, stretched her arms a little and wobbled. I lurched forwards, clutching at the cardboard box which came crashing down, landing with a thud on the bare wooden floor.

'Oh my God, what did you do that for?' she said crossly as she lowered me down.

I picked the box up off the floor and opened it.

'My best hat ruined!'

It was true that the hat was a little damaged by its flight across the living room. The dark felt brim was dented, the black gauze had come unstuck, the dusky silk flower was twisted out of shape.

'Now what am I going to wear to the funeral?' my mother wailed. 'Your Auntie Bessie has high standards you know.'

In the small 1940s Cape Town community of my childhood, funerals, weddings and bar mitzvahs, circumcisions and high holy days were taken seriously from a sartorial point of view. And Mama in particular, with her work as a seamstress, had to put on a good show.

I poked out the dents as best I could and handed her the hat. 'It's OK,' I said. 'Isidore wouldn't mind.'

It wasn't just that my cousin Isidore was dead; in his coffin, he wouldn't be able to see Mama or indeed any of the other women in their funeral finery. But if he'd been alive, he'd have been unconcerned about the hat as well. Isidore didn't notice that kind of thing.

Mama tutted and stomped out of the room, leaving me struggling to button up my shirt and pull on the stiff jacket that I'd only worn once before, for Mikey Cohen's bar mitzvah. Luckily Mama had made it big for me to grow into, so it fitted perfectly now, while for Mikey's great day the sleeves had kept dipping into the salty brine of the gefilte fish. I was going to look all right for Isidore.

'Why did he die, Mama?' I asked for the third or fourth time that day, when I found her sitting at the kitchen table with her head on her arms. The whispered conversations I'd eavesdropped on had left me in doubt.

‘I’ve told you already, it’s not for your ears,’ Mama said. ‘One day when you’re grown-up, perhaps then I’ll tell you the whole story.’

‘Please, Mama. Why can’t you tell me?’

She paused and looked at me darkly. ‘Just wait till you’re older.’

I knew there was something important I was missing out on but there was no point in pressing her. Mama’s lips were shut tight, like an oyster shell. I would have to wait to hear it from her, or get it from other sources. I couldn’t have known then how long that would take.

The last time I saw Isidore was on one of our usual afternoon walks through town, from my home on Main Road, down past Neuberger’s Handyhouse, the synagogue and Irene’s store, past the station, along the dirt path by the railway track and over towards my oupa and ouma’s house, where Isidore would leave me till Mama picked me up in the evening. It was a chance for Mama to get on with her sewing jobs without me under her feet and Isidore always seemed happy to escort me to my grandparents’. He worked early shifts at Uncle Mo’s bakery, so was free to come by after lunch and collect me on his way home, still in his white working clothes, his curly black hair turned grey with flour dust.

I liked those walks with Isidore. He was eighteen or nineteen, the son of my mother’s eldest sister, so the most grown-up of my cousins and far more interesting to me than Fanny Chipped-Tooth, Olga Schmolga or Knock-Kneed Morrie, who were closest to me in age. He didn’t say much, just asked me questions and I, who only had Mama’s nagging and complaints to punctuate my days, was happy to oblige with answers that lasted all the way along Main Road. Now, when I think about it, I wonder how he could have been at all interested in my stories, my fantasies, my small daily furies, when he had so much going on in his own life. But he never showed any signs of anything other than serious attention to the catalogue of petty incidents I put before him. And I never doubted the supremely fascinating nature of my tales.

'Mama said I mustn't talk like that to Morrie it's not nice but Morrie took my Dinky car, the red Cadillac, and won't give it back and his mama says it's his and my mama said stop making a fuss it's just a car and I said it's my favourite one and he said that's mine not yours, you lost yours ages ago and I said no I didn't and he said yes you did, so Mama slapped me round the leg and there was a big red mark, and I'm going to run away next time Mama slaps me, and I'll take some boiled eggs and bread, and Garibaldi biscuits from the jar in the cupboard, and hide them in my pockets, and disappear and never come back, not ever, ever, ever.'

Cousin Isidore nodded. 'It's very bad luck,' he said, smiling a little. 'But don't leave home. Your ma would miss you.'

'Why does Mama always try to make me say sorry when I don't feel sorry at all?'

'That's what mothers are for,' said Isidore. 'She's teaching you what's right and wrong, so that you grow up to be the very best man you can possibly be. She's making a mensch of you.'

'No, she isn't,' I replied straightaway. 'She just doesn't want a fight with Morrie's ma. And Morrie's not going to end up being a mensch the way *he's* going, stealing people's cars.'

Cousin Isidore laughed. 'You're a chochem,' he said. I knew what he meant. A wise man. I'd heard it many times, but usually in Mama's mouth when she was singing the praises of Morrie, with his brilliant marks at school, or Uncle Isaac, who persuaded the bank manager to lend him fifty pounds, invested it in ladies' nylon stockings and ended up with five thousand.

'I reckon you'll end up being a big-noise lawyer or something one day, mensch or not!' Isidore said and he ruffled my hair with his hand and laughed some more.

I laughed too, though I wasn't quite sure what I was laughing at, the idea of being a chochem, or picturing myself swanning around in a lawyer's robes, or just walking along the road enjoying the company of my big cousin Isidore.

After the funeral, for a while I thought a lot about deaths and funerals and Cousin Isidore. I wondered who would come to *my* funeral. It was surprisingly enjoyable, thinking about all the people crying into their hankies and saying things about me that went beyond complaints about not chewing my bread properly, or slurping my chicken soup, or wishing I were a more serious student like Morrie, so I would go on to become a doctor, so useful if someone in the family had a serious ailment. Mama would weep when I was dead, and Fanny, Olga and even Morrie might wish they'd been a bit nicer to me. I wondered whether Isidore had thought the same, or whether the thing that killed him so quickly meant that he hadn't had time to enjoy the thought of dying.

It was strange to think of Isidore dead. I felt sorry for him. He wasn't going to grow up into a proper man and marry and have children and all those things that I had ahead of me if I managed to stay alive longer than Isidore. But most of all I missed our walks, with the Cape Doctor blowing cool and strong, and the daily visit to my grandparents' house that took me out of the stifling heat of our apartment. Now, instead, on weekday afternoons, I had to sit on the sofa and occupy myself quietly, while Mama's sewing-machine needle pecked away at the lengths of material, her feet working the treadle, up and down, up and down. No more walks along Main Road, no one to tell all my little woes to, no small treats at Oupa and Ouma's, no carrot sweets, koeksisters or homentashen. Isidore, by dying, had deprived me of my treats, my lovely afternoons.

As I grew older, I stopped thinking so much about Isidore. Mama's sobs and sighs were soon replaced by other worries and even Aunt Bessie and Uncle Mo rarely talked about him.

One time though, when the whole family was gathered for Passover and we were all crowded round the table in Oupa and Ouma's front room, with its candlesticks and starched white tablecloth and matching plates and silver, there was a little incident that brought Isidore right back into the room with us.

I always looked forward to the highlight of the Passover meal, the hunting of the afikomen, when a piece of matzo bread would be hidden by Oupa and all the children would search the house in the hope of finding it and being given the prize of a little bag of coins, to spend on sweets or toys.

Oupa called for us to start the hunt and off we went, Fanny shrieking with excitement, Olga complaining that it wasn't fair because, being the youngest, she was always pushed out of the way. Morrie set about the task seriously by trying to work out Oupa's psychology. Where would he be most likely to hide it, given where he had hidden it in previous years?

My tactics? I had watched Oupa's movements earlier in the evening and followed him when he'd disappeared to go out to the toilet in the yard. I'd seen him first slip into the back room, with its old mahogany cupboard and bookshelves. I was pretty sure he hadn't noticed me watching. So, when the hunt began, I waited a few moments for the others to start their search, then made straight for the back room. I started looking on the shelves for objects that showed signs of having been disturbed, a vase awkwardly placed, a piece of cloth peeking out of a book, a photo frame tipped up. I flipped through the small collection of books on the shelf – a Hebrew bible, a book of short stories by Sholem Aleichem and a few well-thumbed *Reader's Digest* pamphlets. As I opened the bible, a photograph fell out and landed on the floor. I picked it up and saw that it was of Cousin Isidore. He was leaning against a tree, in an informal pose, smiling out at the camera. Next to him stood another young man, sideways on, his arm slung playfully over Isidore's shoulder. It looked like he might be moving closer towards him, as if any moment he might even snatch a sudden kiss on his cheek. There was something happy about the photograph, something a little sad too. Two young men, on a summer picnic by the river, caught unawares by the camera.

It came as a bit of a surprise to see Isidore looking out at me. I hadn't thought about him for such a long time. He looked just as I remembered him, with his curly black hair, his pale, slender face and his quiet smile.

And then suddenly there was a great yell and Fanny was shouting, 'I've found it! I've found it!' and Olga was crying and Morrie was coming to tell me it was all over; the afikomen had been discovered.

As I came back into the crowded front room, Oupa looked at me sternly, then winked. 'Tricked you there, big mister chochem,' he said, and I blushed guiltily. 'Thought you could work out what I was up to, huh? I wasn't born yesterday!'

'Look what I found though, Oupa,' I said. Fanny may have won the prize but I'd discovered something that I knew would please everyone, a nice reminder of Cousin Isidore, a forgotten photograph that had got lost in the books on the bookshelf, showing him happy, on a picnic with a friend, having a good time.

Oupa took it from me. He picked up his glasses and put them on. He stared at the photograph for a while. Then he took off his glasses and sighed. He passed the photograph to my mama and from her it went slowly around to each of the adults, passing the children by, until it reached Aunt Bessie. She looked at it hard, then placed it carefully on the table, face down. Nothing was said. After a few moments, Oupa went out of the room, taking the photograph with him.

'Time for cake,' my mother said brightly, without looking at me.

'He looks good in the photograph,' I said sadly. 'Just how I remember him from our walks.'

'Yes,' said Mama, 'he does.' She beckoned me over, pulled my face down towards hers and kissed me on the forehead. I wondered why.

'And now for cake,' she said.

Harvey's Wedding

They were heading out on the M1, past Brent Cross and Staples Corner and the web of slip roads and bridges, the computer megastores, Cineworld and self-storage warehouses. They sat quietly, not talking much, as the road sped by. It was a lot to take in; a new life together, a fresh start. Jean asked if she could put on some music and chose some jazz. She sang along, under her breath, a snatch of *Fly Me to the Moon*, and shifted towards him to rest her head on his shoulder. Harvey felt suddenly shy, awkward, not knowing quite what to say, almost as if she were a stranger.

'What did you tell your clients? Did you tell them you were getting married?' he asked.

'No,' she said. 'It seemed a little complicated to explain. I just said I was having a long weekend away.' She paused. 'I think I'll phone Clare, when we stop for a coffee. It'll be about right for Singapore. She'll be getting into work at nine. She'll want to hear how it went.'

He thought about his own son and daughter. He'd spoken to Patrick the night before, tried to give him one last chance to come to the wedding.

'Please, Patrick. It means a lot to me. I'm asking you to do this for me.'

'I'm spending the day with Mum,' Patrick said, his voice quiet, brittle.

Patrick promised to ring him when he got back to London but Harvey wasn't sure that he would. It would take time, he thought. Patrick was like that, slow to get used to new ideas. He'd hated it when they'd taken away his fluffy blanket, when he was three, or when they had tried to leave him at the nursery. And even though it had been his own choice, he'd kicked up a fuss when he'd switched to a college for the sixth form, moping around the house for days and threatening not to go. He liked things to stay the same. But in the end, he always came round.

Lucy was another matter. She had made it perfectly clear many months back that she didn't welcome his calls. 'It's a betrayal, Dad, a fucking betrayal. You've ruined everything,' she'd said, when they'd met in a bar that very last time. And when he'd tried to talk about how people mess up sometimes and do things and then realise that people are getting hurt and then find it hard to unscramble it all, she'd flung back her chair and walked out, leaving a plate of uneaten food, her mobile phone and her coat. He'd run after her to give her the coat and the phone, which she took without a word. My little girl, he found himself saying, my little girl.

Harvey thought about his wedding that morning, a quiet, low-key, registry office affair in Camberwell. His friend Malcolm had acted as best man and Jean's second cousin had agreed, at the last minute, to be a witness. He'd rung a few other friends in the weeks leading up to it but only Malcolm had finally announced himself free. It was disappointing. Malcolm had worked with him at Willards, when he was still in the law. They had occupied the same office but sat back to back, sharing just the space and a waste-paper bin. When Malcolm arrived, moments before the ceremony was due to start, he was wearing the same suit that Harvey remembered from the Willards days, trousers saggy at the knees, shiny from wear and hanging slightly perilously under his belly. He wished that Malcolm had made more effort. 'Just in the nick of time, eh, Harvey?' he wheezed, and Harvey remembered everything he'd disliked about Malcolm and wished he'd had more options for best man. Jean's second cousin, in her sixties, stout and with a pale freckled face, wore an old tweed suit, but at least she had made an effort with the blouse and had worn a flower in her lapel. That was something.

The ceremony was over almost before it had begun. No sooner had they signed the book and shaken hands with the registrar than they were out in the broad paved courtyard, watching the next party arrive. Standing on the slippery paving stones, slick with earlier rain, Harvey held on to Jean and squeezed her arm.

The second wedding party was a large group. The women were dressed in chiffons and silks, pastel creations that floated or billowed or fanned out in the wind. Their hats were large, extravagant affairs, with swirls of ribbon and lustrous sprigs of satin flowers. Some of the men stood a little apart, in a small cluster, watching the women. Harvey noted their admiring gaze. Others laughed loudly, or quickly shared a last cigarette. A smart young man, the groom, stood fidgeting, hands in and out of his pockets, shifting from foot to foot, smoothing back his hair, trying to correct his carnation, which had tipped forward slightly, without damaging the bloom. 'Everything has to be perfect,' Harvey thought.

It was beginning to spit. Clouds were massing in dark slabs of grey and Harvey feared a fresh shower. Jean suggested that it was time they move on. They didn't want to get caught in the rain. But it was good to watch the other wedding, to see the young man nervously fiddling with his carnation and adjusting his tie, to watch the butterfly women on display and to enjoy waiting for the blushing bride. He wanted to see it through to the end, to wait till they emerged from the double doors, man and wife. He knew that they would have confetti, masses of it, showering down in a storm of paper. He knew that there would be champagne corks popping. He knew that there would be cameras flashing and shouts and whoops and lots of applause and he knew that there would be a kiss.

'Let's go somewhere for a drink before the journey,' Jean said, more firmly. Malcolm made his excuses – he had to get back to Willards – but the cousin agreed to join them, before heading off to catch her train. They found a pub called the Goose and Garter, where they sat, the three of them, in the snug, in awkward silence, sipping on warm beer.

And then the cousin was gone too and they were on their own, finishing their beers. Harvey made a silly joke about the goose and garter, something foolish about her wearing the garter so he must be the goose. She smiled. He asked her what time they were booked in at the hotel. She had made the phone call the previous day, checking that dinner could be laid on in their room.

He noticed the way the froth of the beer stayed on her upper lip, giving her a little white moustache. With Molly – and he found himself saying her name aloud in his head for the first time – he'd have teased her and she'd have hit out at him playfully, telling him he should count himself lucky to have any woman at all, moustache or not. He reached across and passed Jean a napkin, so she could wipe it off.

They'd found the car in the side street, looking as they'd left it. No lucky horseshoes, trails of tin cans, sprayed wishes of 'Good luck' or saucy allusions to the pleasures of the night to come. In the boot were the sturdy suitcase he'd already packed and the smaller one she'd brought with her. He wondered what she'd put inside it, whether the silky negligée and underwear she'd worn on that first night would be there, or whether she'd revert to a plainer M&S style. M&S seemed more likely and he found to his surprise that he wouldn't really mind if it were something simple, something befitting the seriousness of the step they'd taken, nothing too frivolous or devil-may-care.

Molly had worn nothing in bed in those early years, no pyjamas or nightdress. In the day she went without a bra and even occasionally knickers – and that had been a thrill, when he wasn't sure and they'd rush home and barely get through the door and when he lifted her dress he'd find her gloriously naked. Later, of course, as everything loosened up a bit, she always wore underwear, so unremarkable that he scarcely noticed it. Certainly nothing you could grace with the name of lingerie.

Now, driving up the M1, with Jean quiet beside him, Harvey's thoughts hurried back once more to Molly, and to his first wedding. They'd got out of bed one morning and decided to do it a week later. Why not, after all? They'd been together for five years, they'd bought a flat together, they wanted kids. Friends had frowned on them for even thinking of it. Marriage is a bourgeois institution, they said. But it had felt like the right thing to do. It was a piece of paper, no more than that, but it was a good piece of paper. He'd secretly taken it out of the desk drawer and looked at it several times in the following days, tracing his fingers over his name, her name, her changed name. She was now, in the nicest possible sense, his. He could feel all right about laying claim to her. Before that he'd been careful, a little fearful that she might take too seriously the whole free love thing, thc ghastly swinging sixties. He was worried she might swing off out of his life. Now he knew they might be together for the duration, if not till death do us part then at least for a good long time. In the end all their friends had pitched up at the registry office, despite their disapproval. Someone had brought crazy foam, party whistles and cheap red wine, and they'd piled onto a Routemaster bus that took them out to Epping Forest, where they found a muddy little spot to spread out a small picnic lunch. Drunk, tired and incredibly happy, in the early hours they found their way back to the flat, where they burrowed down into their double bed and stayed there, till Monday's work and the alarm clock reminded them that the world required more of them than sleep and love.

On the motorway it was raining again, heavily now. Harvey switched on the windscreen wipers. He tried to drag his thoughts back to safer ground. He mustn't keep thinking about Molly, not now of all times. Put her out of his head, at least for today. But there she was, constantly returning, a part of his hard-wiring after thirty years.

He forced himself back to the present and to Jean. They were travelling up to the Peak District for the honeymoon. They'd booked into the Peveril of the Peak, in the village of Thorpe, from where they hoped to do little walks in Dovedale and make a visit to Chatsworth House. It was Jean's choice. He had been a really keen walker in the past, with a mental list of mountains that he ticked off one by one. But for their honeymoon he'd been all for splashing out on something that made more of a statement, an all-inclusive package somewhere far away, like Mexico or Thailand. She'd made it clear she didn't want that and he had respected her wishes. It signalled something about the start they were making, that he would take account of her view. He would be careful. He would do the right thing by her.

The afternoon was wearing on. They stopped for a coffee at a Welcome Break and then set off again towards the north, with the skies darkening and the low fields turning into looming hills. The engine hummed and the road markings hurried by. It was warm in the car and soon she fell asleep. Harvey glanced over at her, really noticing her properly for the first time that day. She was dressed in a smart cream suit, her jacket open to show a pink silk blouse. Her blond hair was freshly cut, in a neat bob. He realised that he hadn't ever asked her whether it was dyed or not. Probably not, he thought, but he was no expert in these things. She was an attractive woman, her face young for her years, surprisingly unlined. Her figure was also good, full but not too full.

In all that time with Molly, he'd looked at other women and wondered if he'd missed out in any way, his entire adult life having been spent with just one woman. But he'd stayed faithful to her and had never really been seriously ted, not even in the early years with that pretty secretary at Willards. Jean, however, had been different. They'd got to know one another through work, become friends, and then she'd let him know that she was interested and he had found that hard to resist. He had gone with the flow and it had been utterly thrilling, intoxicating. Another set of intimacies, a breaking of old patterns, trying out a different life, like an actor buttoning himself into a new costume – a last chance to play the young prince. But it had become complicated. Christ, he was no expert in these things and, as he discovered, much better at simple stories than messy ones. Molly had found out in an entirely clichéd way – reading a text message on his phone – and after the screaming and shouting and the tears, she'd made it clear that forgiveness wasn't an option. 'I don't think I can give you up,' he'd said to her, 'but I can't let Jean down either.' Molly had simply said, 'Fuck you.'

Perhaps if he'd been able to tell her that it was just a fling, she'd have come round in the end. Maybe if he'd sworn there and then never to see Jean again, she'd have been able to make an accommodation, lick her wounds and recover. But he'd tried to be honest. 'Somehow or other, I've got involved,' he said.

It was only a week or so later, when he was sitting with all his belongings in the transit van he'd hired for the day, that he realised this was it. The end. He drove straight to Jean's flat and was propelled into a new beginning. And it wasn't long after the divorce that Jean had broached the subject of marriage. Her desire for security, squaring things with her ageing mother, making it legal. It wasn't a big deal, she'd said. Only if he wanted to. 'Of course,' he'd said straightaway. 'If it'll make you happy.'

He looked over at Jean now as she slept in the car and felt touched by her childish flush, her hair flopped over her brow, the way she blew the breath out of her mouth in a soft little snore. He thought about all her qualities, what he'd discovered about her since they'd been together. She was honest, affectionate, kind. She was lovely, a really lovely person. And she was a good-looking woman, no doubt about it. She made the best of herself. She looked just fine.

And then all at once, and taking him by surprise with its sudden force, it was no good any more. None of it. He couldn't do this thing. He couldn't do it. He couldn't stop thinking about Molly. He couldn't stop himself. It wasn't fine. None of it was fine. And Jean wasn't fine either. He thought of his wedding, the first one, sitting on the top deck of the Routemaster as it wound through Wood Green, Edmonton and Walthamstow. He thought of his wedding today, with Malcolm and the second cousin, the four of them standing, damp and bedraggled, in the rain, and of the other wedding with the confetti and the kiss. He watched the darkness falling and the looming hills and he wanted to cry out or smash the windscreen or turn the wheel and head off in another direction. He wanted to talk to his children. He wanted to ring their old friends Nick and Caroline, whom he hadn't spoken to for so long. He wanted to be sitting in the front room, reading his paper, while Molly cooked for their friends. He wanted to get drunk with them all and laugh about the bloody stupid things *another* man had done and what a crazy fool that man had been to lose everything for a ridiculous bit of stupidity. Men! Brains in their cocks! He wanted to be able to throw up his hands with his friends and say 'Men!' Just like that. And to laugh out loud. He thought of the night ahead in the Peveril of the Peak in Thorpe, and more than anything he wanted to go home to Molly, and end up in bed with her, that night and the next night and the next. Easy as that. Simple as that. Simple. Part of his hard-wiring.

As they came off the motorway, he pulled into a lay-by. Jean stirred and looked at him briefly but then turned in her seat and went back to sleep. He sat still, looking at his hands. For some moments he sat like that, afraid to move. Then quietly he opened the door and got out of the car. She was stirring again, perhaps waking properly to find out why they had stopped, what was going on. He was walking away from the car. He was pretending it was a toilet stop. He was waving back at her. He was smiling at her and waving, making pointing signals towards his trousers to indicate that it was just a toilet stop, just that. He was smiling. Looking back, he saw her adjusting her make-up in the little vanity mirror on the sunshade. He carried on walking to the end of the lay-by. When he was right at the end he stopped. He checked back and saw that she was combing her hair. She was applying her lipstick. She looked relaxed. Perhaps she was thinking about the meal the hotel was laying on for them and wondering whether there'd be flowers and champagne. Maybe she was thinking about Clare in Singapore or about the refurbishment of the new flat they had bought together in Camden. She looked up and smiled. She trusted him. She was his wife now, to have and to hold. From this day forth. He stood there for a long moment, the dark sky and the rain beating down on him, London and the motorway behind, the mountains ahead.

My Man

Brian is snoring beside me. He's slumped in the seat, head tipped back, the empty burger packet lying greasy on his lap, the can of Fanta dribbling the last of its sticky sweetness out onto his jeans. Serves him right for falling asleep on the job, I think, though he'll be narked as hell when he wakes up. And you can be pretty sure it'll be me who'll get the blame. No word of thanks for keeping an eye on things, for getting the job done.

'You doughnut,' I rehearse in my head. 'When can I ever rely on you for a thing?'

'Shut up, wanker. Leave off, birdbrain.' That'll be him. No finesse. Can't even do verbal abuse with style.

I rub my eyes and peer at my watch. 4.30 a.m. I look up at the house. Four storeys of fresh cream paintwork and fancy columns. Big windows stretching across the whole terrace. Primrose Hill Georgian. Expensive. Surprisingly tasteful for a man like him. Not the usual suburban mock something or other. There's a little sliver of light where my man hasn't quite got the curtains to meet. Usually he's pretty good at avoiding that. Obsessive he is, though how he thinks anyone'd get a good view from that angle, God only knows. No nicely placed trees to shimmy up or anything.

He's obviously still up and partying, my man. And no one's come out yet either. Frank, Mikey, Gianluigi, Darren, the lads, all still there. And the girls as well, the ones who piled out of the car with them, when the nightclub closed. Blonde number one, wobbly with champagne or maybe just struggling on the cobblestones in her Jimmy Choos. Number two, fake tan not quite making it as far as the hard little imitation boobs spilling out of her black mini dress. Numbers three and four, Lulu and Maya from *So You Think You Can...* , and that cheap bird, Charlene McGuire, who got thrown off the show for shagging the producer and getting caught. Slag.

I yawn. How much longer can they keep this up? My camera's parked on the dashboard, ready for action. And Brian – who's supposed to be my partner – is dead to the world. Unusual, him and me, working as a team. Most of the guys are on their own. Out for themselves. But then we'd got to know each other over the years, shoving and barging to get the best view, exchanging every insult under the sun, then running to the newsagent's next morning to see who'd got the best shot, secretly having to admit that sometimes it was him, sometimes me. The occasional drink in the pub when we'd both got what we'd come for and run it down to Fleet Street.

There was one long job that finally made us come up with the idea of pooling our talents. Two days of watching, holed up on a country lane, waiting for Lord Doodah to appear out of his cosy little nest with his ladylove. And

Brian is standing shivering in the trees and he says to me, 'Tell you what, I'll do you a favour and you do me one. I'll have a quick half-hour kip in my car, pop down to the local pub for a piddle in a proper facility, get myself a hot meal and you cover for me. I'll take your second-best shot if our lovers decide to make a showing. That'll do me fine. Then when I'm refreshed and all that, I'll nip back and take over and you can have a bit of a break yourself.'

'Done,' I says. 'It's a deal.' When I got back Lord Muck was still locked in there, snuggled up with his sultry señorita, but the die was cast. Brian and I started doing each other little favours whenever our paths crossed. Life became cushy. In the end, it wasn't just the odd pee in a toilet instead of a bush. I once even managed to get myself a whole weekend away for my kid brother's stag do and still got the picture slapped on my editor's desk in time for the next morning's front page.

'Great shot, Bill. One of your best! You're really hitting your stride these days.'

Of course, that was a few years back when Brian was right on form. He takes it all a bit for granted these days, now that he knows I'll cover his lazy backside. He gets a good night's kip while I'm left propping open my eyelids.

But then it's hard to wake someone when they're looking like he is now. His top lip's vibrating in time with the snores. You can see the little pearls of sweat, caught on the stubble just below his nose. His hair, quite a decent thatch for a man of his age, is sticking up to one side, and his chest is going up and down like a battered old accordion wheezing out a creaky old tune. Who'd have the heart to wake him?

I'm looking at him and wondering what I'm getting out of this arrangement these days when I catch a little movement over the street. Is this it? A bit of action at last? The door opens and out rolls Darren, one bird on either arm. I pick up the camera and take a few shots, but just out of habit. Darren's not what I'm after. Him and the girls are small fry by comparison with my man.

A few minutes later, Gianluigi and Mikey slip quietly out of the door, collars up, dark glasses, heads down. Too late, guys. I've already got you. But there's no need to worry. It's not you I'm after, either. A car draws up, a black limousine. Like a sleek black cat of the night the limo purrs and pulls away and they're gone. I congratulate myself on my nice metaphorical flourish. I'll mention it to Brian when he wakes up, though I can't expect much appreciation from him.

'A limo's a limo, Bill,' he'll say. 'Did you nail the shot?'

Back at the house it's five down, four to go. And him. My man. Alfie Lorrimer, Player of the Year, marked down on Bottomley's list for the England top job next season. Married to Desirée. A star couple, top of the paps' hit list.

'Get us something good on Lol and Desi and you'll be able to put your feet up, Bill, retire to a villa on the Costa del Sol!' Lawrence White, the editor, says to me.

He's a big party animal is Lolly, we all know that, but up until now that's as far as it goes. Nothing juicy to pin on him or his missus. The team closes ranks, whenever there's a sniff of anything untoward. But I'm ever the optimist and this time it was looking like my luck might be in, what with Desi off on tour in the US of A and Alfie off the leash, out clubbing with the boys. But as his mates disappear, one by one, into the night, I see my fat pension cheque being torn up before my eyes.

It's twenty minutes since Mikey and Gianluigi have drifted off and I'm still sitting there, bolt upright, damned if I'm going to miss something after such a long wait. Brian has gone quiet. He's turned in his seat. His head is lolling to one side, a thin dribble of spit falling sideways from the corner of his mouth, onto my car-seat upholstery. He's an animal is Brian. I'll make him pay for the valeting one day, to get rid of the years of accumulated burger fat and body fluids he's left on my Volvo.

I'm just thinking of getting out of the car to get a different angle when the door opens and out comes Charlene. And then straight after, there's the unknown bird in the Jimmy Choos and her friend with the boobs. They set off down the road laughing and I get a good few shots out the open side window. Not worth much though, unless you want to treat yourself to the sight of three fake blondes showing a bit of leg on the streets of London.

That's it then, I think. All the blondes safely out the house. In town without the missus and he's behaving himself like a perfect gent, more's my misfortune. Sweet FA. I laugh at my joke. Another one for Brian to ignore, when he makes his return journey from the land of Nod.

Just Frankie left now, and my man. Teammates, best buds. Perhaps he'll stay over, keep Lol company while Desi's away. I'm already thinking, That's it, Bill, you're done now, time to make tracks. May as well pack up and go home. I've got in my head the nice cup of tea I'll make, the toast and Marmite, then straight into bed to catch up on some sleep. I'm putting my camera on the back seat of the car and I'm screwing the cup back on the thermos. I'm getting ready to give Brian a shove and tell him we're off.

And then the cream front door opens, just a crack. I grab the camera again and wind down the window of the Volvo. The front door shuts again, fast. Someone who was going out has changed their mind. Perhaps they're stopping for a bit more of a chat. I jump out the car and leg it across the road, then pull up sharp and tiptoe carefully up to the door. The letterbox is big, shiny, polished, with a heavy knocker, a Rolex of the door furniture world. Slowly I bend down. Quietly I lift the heavy brass flap and peer inside.

No one in the hall. Nothing. Lights on. Silence. I'm looking up the stairs, to see if they've gone up there. I'm looking beyond the hall, towards a room at the back of the house, a snug or TV room or something by the looks of it. Nothing to see. I'm scanning the banister and the hall table for something, anything.

And then suddenly they appear from a side door, coming out of the living room, and they're right there, under my nose, Frankie and Lol. I'm holding the letterbox open with one hand and fumbling around for my camera with the other. And oh my God, that's not the only fumbling that's going on. Oh my God, just wait till you see what I'm getting, Brian. This is it. The big one. While you're snoring away in the Volvo I'm getting that house in the Costa del Sol signed and sealed. I ease the camera towards the letterbox and click, click, click, I'm getting the best pictures of my life. They'll be a bit rough – not the greatest light, not the best angle – but hey! My man and Frankie, hands all over each other in the front hall. Lol and Frankie Find Their True Form. When Desi's Eyes Are Off the Ball, Lolly Scores.

I'm clicking away and hoping for more. Go for it, boys. Do the business right there on the carpet in the front hall.

But no, they're edging back into the living room. It's all over, at least for me and my Canon, but I've got plenty, enough to put a nice fat cheque in my pocket. I put the cap on the lens and hurry down the stone steps and onto the pavement.

But then I stand there for a moment. Brian's still slumped in his seat, dead to the world. My sleeping partner. And it strikes me, all of a sudden, that I don't have to tell him. I could just get in the car, take out the keys, start up the ignition and drive us off home. 'Not worth staying any longer,' I could say. 'No action tonight, mate.' Why should I do all the work and share the proceeds with a dosser like Brian?

I stand a while longer, thinking, then I walk over to the car and open the door.

Brian's just coming to.

'What? What?' he mumbles. 'What's going on?'

I climb into the driver's seat, shut the door and look at him, yawning, rubbing the sleep out of his eyes, looking a bit lost, like a little boy, half wondering where the hell he is. I put my camera down. I take off my jacket. I breathe deeply.

And then I let out a whoop that could wake the whole neighbourhood. I put my hand on that thatch of greying hair of his and ruffle it affectionately. I take his face, stubbled and sticky and still smelling faintly of Fanta and chip fat, in both my hands, and I pull him towards me and I give him one enormous kiss, full throttle, right on the lips. And he's looking like I've taken leave of my senses. And he's laughing nervously. 'What are you doing for Christ's sakes?' And I'm thinking to myself, Bill Walters, me old mate, that was the best kiss of your entire fucking life.

The Dating Game

They agreed to meet in a café in a small turning off Marylebone High Street. It was her favourite place, an old-fashioned establishment where tea was served in china cups and the menu offered cream cakes and glossy iced patisserie. The clientele was mainly older women meeting for tea, mothers taking children out for a treat, or men in tweed jackets. It was safe. Knowing that Walter, the friendly, middle-aged owner, was there, bustling around in the background, was a reassurance.

The description had been reasonable enough:

Playful Prof

Professor of Law, in his early sixties, widower, theatre and music lover, seeks companion to share leisure time. Youthful, sincere, tactile, with a good sense of humour.

But of course, Playful Prof turned out to be anything but. As usual, he was more late sixties than early, his hair thinning, his skin a little loose and wrinkled like that of a tortoise; he had more in common with the elderly tweed-jacketed men who made up much of the café's daytime clientele than with the young, sprightly man of her imagination. When she walked up to his table, dressed in her best camel coat and wearing her uncomfortable, but stylish, new shoes, she saw the instant look of disappointment on *his* face. He'd also been hoping for something different, she could see. For 'tactile' read 'randy', she thought. Perhaps that photograph she'd had taken in a studio did make her look a little more buxom and inviting than was strictly the case. She'd seen that sudden look of surprise more than once now and wondered whether she should replace the photo with the earlier one she'd used, taken out in the garden, of her standing in her jeans, her hair a little ruffled by the wind.

They ordered tea and cakes. Luckily the ordering took up some time, the selection of cakes being impressive enough to require separate trips to the counter to choose. They managed to go through the motions quite satisfactorily, asking about each other's children, previous or dead partners or wives, careers, interest in theatre and music. Both being passionate about Shakespeare, both loving Bach didn't seem to take them very far, though on paper it should have done, and his good sense of humour seemed to have deserted him on this occasion. Long before they finally asked for the bill she'd realised he was a non-starter and supposed that he felt the same.

They shook hands politely and said goodbye on the pavement, neither of them suggesting another date, and then she remembered her umbrella and went back in to collect it. Over at last, she thought with relief.

‘He wasn’t right for you,’ said Walter, patting her on the shoulder as he edged past her to clear a table. ‘Much too old. And no joie de vivre.’

Yes, she thought. Not playful enough.

❖

Warm William

Optician, aged 58, (divorced) with 3 children, seeks genuine, intelligent woman with good sense of humour. Enjoys cooking, eating out and visits to galleries and museums. Wants to put a bit of magic back into his life. Not bad looking, according to friends.

She was a bit early this time, so she found a table near the front of the café, where he would be able to pick out the camel coat and red scarf she had promised she would be wearing. Walter spotted her, sitting there nervously, patting down her hair and applying a fresh layer of lipstick. He waltzed over, tray in hand.

‘Ah, Miss Veronica,’ he said, greeting her as he always did, in terms that would have made her hackles rise were it anyone else, but from his mouth sounded respectful and friendly. ‘A new man today, is that right?’

‘’Fraid so. I’m not sure I have high hopes of this one though. He’s an optician. But he did sound nice. Warm, he said.’

‘Ah, warm. Yes, warm is good. And an optician... It would save you a lot of bills on your glasses.’

She laughed. ‘I could get those varifocals I’ve been promising myself all these years!’

She asked for a glass of water while she was waiting, then sat watching the door anxiously.

Twenty minutes later, she saw him, William, hovering outside on the pavement, adjusting his coat, smoothing his hair. She recognised him from the photo. It had been accurate. He looked as suggested, reasonably attractive for a man of his age. Her spirits lifted and her slight irritation at his lateness subsided.

When he came over to the table, she stood up and reached out to shake his hand. It was trembling and his fingers brushed her own only lightly. Joe, her ex-husband, had a handshake that was firm and strong. She often found herself matching them up to Joe, these men. It was stupid and annoying but she couldn't help it. Sometimes she was looking for more of the same, sometimes less, but she couldn't ever say which it would be, until the very moment it happened. Face to face, however, it became immediately obvious. In this case, William needed a firm handshake, like Joe's. This one just wouldn't do.

It was difficult when she'd decided something like that in the very first moments of meeting someone. She'd known this about William straightaway and now she had to sit chatting, albeit perfectly amiably, about his house, his children, his work, his interests. He was just what he'd said – a nice, caring man, a little nervous perhaps, but warm. He would make someone a very good partner. But not her. Chemistry had not been her best subject in school but she was highly skilled in knowing when it was wrong.

'Shall we meet up again?' he asked cheerfully when they'd drained their cups and picked up the last of the crumbs of cake with their forks.

'That would be lovely,' she said, knowing full well that when he called she would find some excuse and a way to let him down gently. It would be too cruel to say something now.

He offered his hand again, this time more strongly, but by now it was too late, and off he went, leaving her to collect her things together. I think I'll stay and have another cup of tea, she said to herself. Gather my thoughts before heading home.

Walter was busy, so his daughter, Rosalie, came over but she didn't say anything. Just raised one eyebrow and smiled sympathetically. Walter waved though, as she left, and gave her a similarly sympathetic look.

❖

Veronica decided to let things lie for a week or two. It was exhausting, manufacturing a love life. Much easier to drift on. After all, it wasn't as if she was actively unhappy without a man. She had lots of friends and plenty to do. It was just that there was a little space in her life that wasn't filled. The sudden wish to touch someone, to have them stroke her face, or tell her how lovely she was, left a gap. She was loved by many, she knew that. But adored by none.

Her marriage with Joe had ended disastrously but she realised, even in those final days, when they'd decided to end it all, that there was still a little bit of her that *was* adored. A pity he had been unable to stop himself loving so many other women as well. Monogamy hadn't suited him. But probably, if she could have put up with that, he'd have been very happy to continue as they were, giving her quite a large slice of his affection, if not the whole cake.

It had taken a year or so, after the divorce, for her to face up to the fact that she wasn't going to meet anyone at work or on the usual social round of dinner parties with her married friends. Someone suggested the internet and told her a story about a friend who had a friend whose friend had found a partner that way. And once she'd overcome the initial aversion to something so calculated and lacking in spontaneity, she set to the task with her customary efficiency. Usually it was her responding to the ads from men, rather than them responding to hers. That was the way supply and demand went, so she discovered. Presentable men over fifty were much sought-after; they could take their pick. Presentable women were available in abundance and struggled even to get a flicker of interest.

But then, one day, she opened her inbox and there was a message from another man, asking to meet up. She looked at his profile. The photograph was really rather appealing. He had wrinkles, yes, and his hair was grey but his eyes had a bit of a twinkle and whoever had photographed him had caught him with a convincing smile, a little half-ironic grin that seemed to say, 'Oh my God I'm being photographed for a dating site. Isn't that crazy?' It was the look she'd have had on her photo had she not been trying so very hard to seem sexy and younger than her years.

He was a history teacher, a head of department, in a secondary school. His profile said he'd been single for a while, having come out of a relationship that had lasted several years. His interests? The usual, nothing out of the ordinary, except that he said he had a passion for everything to do with Italy and loved travelling there during his long school holidays. In the email he said he'd noticed that she spoke Italian and had lived and worked in Bologna for two years. He thought perhaps they might have that in common.

She didn't wait before replying but sent a quick message back saying she'd be very pleased to talk to him. First impressions over the phone were good; he had a cheerful, attractively deep voice – 'sonorous', she described it as to herself afterwards, with 'a warm timbre'. She agreed to meet him. How did Walter's café in Marylebone sound for the following Saturday afternoon?

A week later and there she was, sitting at her favourite table waiting for Hopeful Historian to arrive. Walter came over to see if she wanted anything.

'No thanks, Walter. I'm meeting another potential suitor. I'll wait and order with him.'

'Nice jacket,' he said. 'New?'

'Yes. I didn't think the camel coat was quite right for this one. And I've always wanted a brown leather jacket, so I splashed out.'

'It suits you. He'd better be worth it!'

She smiled at the compliment; it felt good to have Walter's approbation. 'I've got a great feeling about this one. All the right vibes,' she said. 'Maybe something will come of it.'

He shrugged his shoulders. 'Maybe I'm just a bit old-fashioned or something but for me, I couldn't do this online dating thing. When I met Rosalie's mother, it was like in a movie. Her eyes flashed at me and that was that. I had no idea who she was or what she did. I found out later. But by that time, she could have been a thief or a street-sweeper for all I cared. Nothing would have stood in my way.'

'Walter, I didn't know what an old romantic you were. Love at first sight!'

'Oh yes, just ask Rosalie about me and her mother. We were like two turtle doves.' He sighed.

She wanted to ask him more but her quick glance at her watch sent him straight back behind the counter with his tray of dirty plates.

'Good luck this time. I hope he's the right one.'

When Hopeful Historian came in he was also wearing a brown leather jacket, but faded and comfortable-looking, with a narrow red scarf round his neck.

'Snap,' he said and she laughed.

She stood up.

'Veronica?'

'Michael?'

He hesitated slightly then kissed her once on the cheek.

'Mike actually,' he said. 'Only my headteacher calls me Michael. When she's cross.'

They sat down together, as if held on shared strings by a skilful puppeteer. He chose the cheesecake, densely smooth and not too dauntingly large, baked in a rich pastry shell.

'Good choice,' she said. 'Walter's speciality!'

She chose a shiny chocolate éclair.

'Not a dieter then!' and after a little pause, 'Thank God.'

It wasn't long before they tried out their Italian.

'Wow, I'm impressed,' he said.

'So am I. I thought I'd forgotten it all. But I suppose it's all in there somewhere, buried, just waiting to be dug up.'

Like me, she thought. 'I haven't spoken it properly for such a long time, not really since Bologna.'

She felt a pang when she thought of that time in Bologna before meeting Joe, everything ahead of her, just waiting to happen – love, marriage, children, home, happiness. It all seemed assured. Che sarà, sarà. What will be will be. Now here she was, just turned fifty-three, divorced, no children, lonely, unattached. What would be *had* been, and although there had been lots of good times, there wasn't much left to show for it all.

'Thinking of Italy?' he said.

'Remembering Bologna. I was just twenty-two. It was wonderful. I had a ball.'

'Plenty pasta!' he said in a fake Italian accent and they laughed and her spirits lifted again.

Now they talked easily and the time passed quickly. Walter brought over a fresh pot of tea and gave her a little wink. She hoped Mike hadn't noticed. She wondered what Walter thought of him. Did the wink suggest approval?

As often happened on these dates, they left the more serious questions till the end – her divorce, his broken relationship, trying again in your fifties. They agreed to talk again on the phone, perhaps meet again soon. He looked at his watch, reached for his jacket and stood up. 'I've really enjoyed meeting you,' he said. 'We seem to have lots in common!' He leaned across the table and kissed her, on both cheeks this time, and then, all too quickly, he was gone.

Walter came speeding over. 'Two kisses! I think you've scored a hit!'

She found herself blushing. Like a teenager, she thought. Theatrically, she took up her paper serviette and fanned her face with it. 'Just feeling a little hot,' she said. And then, 'I think this calls for a fresh cup of tea.' It was quiet in the café, so he came and sat down and joined her and they toasted her chances of romance this time round.

When Mike hadn't called by Wednesday her hopes fell. She perched on a chair near the phone, picked it up a few times, then put it down again. Bloody hell, she thought. What nonsense is this, sitting waiting by a telephone for a man to call?

She thought she'd take her mind off things with a walk in the park. The sun was out and the whole of North London seemed to have had the same idea. The park was heaving with walkers, dogs, children, bikes and trikes, pushchairs and prams. She passed a young man and girl sitting on a bench snogging. Their bodies were twisted together in a snake-like coil, arms and legs, necks and faces interlocked. They'd shut the world out, oblivious to curious stares. Further ahead, an elderly couple, in stiff walking boots and thick jackets, were taking a slow path up the hill. She looked more spry than him, her sturdy legs making easier work of the steep incline. As he paused for breath, she turned towards him and locked her arm in his, to help him along. Veronica walked past the little café, where the owner had put out his round outdoor tables to let people catch the first of the spring sunshine. The tables seemed to be full of couples of all ages, out for a morning stroll and coffee.

Couples everywhere! she thought. I'm incapable of seeing anything else these days. Tunnel vision.

On the way home, she moseyed around for a bit, looking in the Oxfam shop, where she found an exceptionally nice grey cashmere jumper that looked as if it had hardly been worn. The assistant knew her well by now.

'Lovely that, isn't it? It'll go well with those grey trousers you found last week. And the camel coat. You've got a good eye, you have!'

She stopped off at Walter's to buy a tart to take to her mother's as a little treat – Lois loved Walter's pastries. It was quiet in the café. She watched him packaging up the tart, assembling the box and neatly tying it with a thin strand of raffia. His hands were dextrous. She noticed their broadness, the fineness of his fingers, as he worked.

'How's the love life?' Walter asked.

'Oh, you know, so-so.'

'I don't like to ask but did he...?'

'Not yet. Still waiting.'

'It's only Wednesday,' he said. 'Maybe he's been busy at work?'

'Maybe.'

'You know these teachers. No time in the week for anything but work. All those naughty children. And so much marking.'

'True,' she said more brightly.

'I was a teacher once, you know.'

'I didn't know that, Walter.'

'In a primary school. That's where I met Rosalie's mother. She came to teach singing at my school.'

'So how did you end up in London?'

'I had to move from Hungary when Sophia died. Rosalie was still quite small and my mother-in-law was in London, so I came here. She looked after Rosalie in the day and I got work – whatever I could find.'

'I'm sorry, Walter. I didn't know.'

'Oh, it's a long time ago now. I'm happy enough. Running my own business. My own boss. And look at Rosalie too! A proper English girl now. It was a good decision to come here.'

Two young men came in and sat down at a table, swiftly followed by an older woman and her Scottish terrier, who yapped round Veronica's legs.

'I'd better let you get on,' she said to Walter, though she would have liked to hear more about his early life with Sophia.

'Good luck with your history teacher. I'm sure he'll phone!'

Veronica strolled home. She thought about Walter. She hadn't realised how much he'd been through. But now, despite it all, here he was on his own, and seemingly managing fine. It was cheering to think of that. You *could* survive on your own into middle age. Though of course he did have Rosalie – someone to love and give him love, and a lasting link to his wife. It was touching to think of him keeping faithful to his feelings for Sophia, for all those years.

That evening, when she got back from her mother's, the phone rang. It was Mike.

'Veronica? I'm phoning to see if you'd like to meet up.'

'Sure. Of course. That would be very nice.' She tried to keep the wobble out of her voice.

'A meal out this time maybe? Carluccio's in Hampstead? The Italian connection and all that?'

'Lovely.'

'Saturday night?'

'Ummm. Let me just check in my diary.'

'Or Friday if not?'

'No Saturday's fine.'

'Saturday it is then. Super. Meet you there at eight.'

She put down the phone. She could hear her pulse beating loudly in her ears. This dating game was no joke. Bad enough for a sixteen-year-old but bloody well impossible when you were into your fifties. One minute you're the sad little wallflower sitting watching the action from the edge and the next you find yourself out there dancing with the best bloke in the room.

She jumped up and down a few times, just to confirm to herself how excited she was. Who could she tell? Apart from Walter and Rosalie, she'd kept it strictly under wraps. She didn't want her friends gossiping, especially if nothing came of it. Her mother? Absolutely not. Lois definitely wouldn't approve.

The next morning, after pretending to work at the computer for an hour or two, she grabbed her coat and headed for the café.

'Not really here to buy anything,' she said sheepishly. 'I just wanted to tell you my news.' She knew that she had an absurd little grin on her face but it was hard to banish.

'He called?'

'Yep! How did you guess?'

'By your face. You look... ' He searched for the word. 'Radiant, that's the right word isn't it?'

'Well, yes. It feels nice to be wanted. A bit of life in the old bird yet.'

'I'm very pleased for you.'

They stood a little awkwardly. She wasn't buying anything. He had nothing more to say. She tried to think of something new to add, to keep the conversation going, but nothing came to her.

'Well, I'll be off then,' she said.

'Come in for a coffee soon. On the house.'

She thanked him and smiled, then turned to go. But before she left she said, 'Walter, can I ask you something? Do you still miss your wife very much? Is it hard for you, being alone?'

He looked embarrassed. Perhaps she'd been too personal, overstepped the mark. She was just a customer, after all.

'I'm not always so very alone, you know. I've had women friends from time to time over the years. I've not been lonely. In fact, there is someone I'm getting to know now. At my art class. Maybe something will happen. Who knows?'

'Oh,' Veronica said, 'I'm glad.' She felt the blood rush to her face. 'Must go,' she said and waved to him as she went.

Walking back down Marylebone High Street she found herself thinking about Walter. So, he had a potential girlfriend. At his art class. That was a surprise. She had been so sure that he lived on his own, with just Rosalie for female company. She'd never imagined him anywhere other than at the café. In her mind he was always drying cups or laying tables, making coffee or serving cakes. She'd never considered what he did after he turned the sign to closed and pulled down the blinds. An art class indeed. And a woman. She hurried past the Oxfam shop. She should be thinking about what to wear for her date with Mike. But somehow her mood had changed.

The date with Mike went very well. He was surprisingly relaxed, which calmed her nerves, and they talked freely. The osso buco was good, the Montepulciano even better, and by the end of the evening she was feeling that maybe something might come of this. She was moderately attracted to him and he clearly fancied her. When he reached over for the wine his hand managed to brush against hers and she noticed his gaze following her closely when, after the dessert, she excused herself to go to the toilet. Looking at herself in the mirror and adjusting her hair before re-joining him, she wondered what would happen next. Would he suggest a coffee at his place, or at hers? And what would she do? Say yes and follow through on all that implied? Or politely refuse and hope he wouldn't take it as a rebuff but rather a sign that she was just taking things slowly? She wondered what Walter would say if she told him.

'Coffee?' Mike said, as she returned from the toilet. 'Here? Or at your place maybe? Or mine?'

It was laughable. Such a predictable code but absolutely essential. She couldn't blame him; how else would the wheels turn? If he'd suggested an ice cream or a walk through the park or going on to a late bar that would have been more ambiguous. Coffee was clear. But what about no to coffee? Not yet, or not at all?

He was sitting waiting for her response, a little bashful, a little nervous. What should she say? She had to decide.

❖

Sunday. The day after her date with Mike. A beautiful day, windy but warm. Trees shaking their pale blossom down over the paths, insects dancing around pollen-filled blooms, the grass of Regent's Park splashed with picnic blankets and bodies stretched out on towels. She had come out for a walk in the late afternoon, alone. Her regular Sunday-lunchtime visit to Lois over, and her flat feeling empty and silent, she wandered out into the park and found herself a bench to sit on and think.

Four thirty. What time did Walter close up for the afternoon? Was it four on a Sunday, or five? She wasn't sure. Could she go and talk to Walter about what had happened? She'd known him a long time, yes, but just to chat to in the café. He was friendly to all the customers, not just her. The banter probably livened up his day and he was good at it; it brought him a loyal following. She took out her book and tried to read. The page remained unturned, the words unread, as her brain whirred.

Quarter to five. If she got up now, she could do a brisk walk through the park and perhaps reach the café before it closed. She'd be able to catch him clearing up and cheerfully intimate to him what had happened and hear what he had to say. But no. She'd stay and enjoy the sunshine. She'd read her book. She'd be sensible. There was no hurry. Next week would do. She could pop in then for a coffee and fill him in on what had happened on her date.

Ten to five. She closed her book. No use pretending to read any more. She stuffed it into her bag and got up to stroll on through the park. But now she was hurrying. In fact, she was beginning to trot. Slow down, for God's sake, she told herself, but she was picking up speed and, despite the wind, found herself sweating with the effort of running as fast as she could down Marylebone High Street, towards the café.

By the time she got there she was red in the face and her T-shirt was sticking to her. A trickle of sweat ran down her back and another down between her breasts. Closed. The little sign was turned around and the blinds were down. Written on the glass were the opening times, Sundays 10.00 a.m. to 4.00 p.m. It had been closed for ages. She felt the tears coming. 'My God, I've been an idiot,' she said out loud. 'A bloody fool.'

She wiped her face on her arm and waited to get her breath back, leaning on the window for support.

At that moment the door of the café opened and Walter emerged, jacket on, carrying a bag, clearly locking up and on his way out.

'Veronica?' he said, looking surprised. 'Are you OK?'

'Yes, just a bit hot,' she said.

'Something bad happen?'

'Not really. Well, actually, yes, in a way.'

He took her arm. 'Come in and sit down. I'll get you a glass of water.'

He unlocked the door and guided her in. It was cool in the café, with the blinds pulled down and the light dim. She sat at the nearest table while he went behind the counter and poured her a glass of water. He came and sat down opposite her and waited patiently till she was ready to talk.

'I'm really sorry to bother you, Walter. I've just got myself in a bit of a state about this dating business. The history teacher, Mike, he's a nice chap and I think he likes me. The date was fine, we got on well, it felt OK...' Her words trailed away.

'But?'

'I don't want to be on my own any more – I'm lonely and it makes me sad. But when it came to it, I just couldn't bring myself to take it any further with him. I wanted to – oh how I wanted to make it work, but it didn't feel right. OK is not good enough. It has to be something more than that. I told him I didn't think I wanted to see him again.'

'And?'

'He accepted it graciously and we agreed to go our separate ways.'

'And now you're upset?'

'Yes, but not about him. I'm glad I told him how I felt – it was the right thing to do. I think I've been rather silly. You were right to be doubtful about this whole online dating business. I've been looking for romance in all the wrong places.'

There was a moment of silence. It felt awkward to her, and very long, as if she were a character caught in a slow-motion scene in a not-very-good film. Walter looked at her intently and she at him. His face was sympathetic, friendly, kind as usual. She couldn't read more into it.

'Enough of me,' she said, trying to sound breezy. 'How about you and the woman at the art class?' It was hard to get the edge out of her voice, to make it seem like a simple change of tack.

'We went out yesterday for the first time.'

Ah.

'And?'

'She's nice. I like her.'

There was another pause.

'Good,' she said, and then, 'Well,' beginning to move, starting to collect her things.

'Well.'

'You were just locking up. I probably shouldn't keep you.'

'Are you all right now?'

'Yes. Fine.'

He steered her out of the café gently, his hand resting on her shoulder. It made every nerve in her body stand up and shout out.

He shut and locked the door behind him. Then they stood on the street, shuffling awkwardly, trying to find suitable words.

'Thank you,' she said, 'for being so kind.' Should she shake his hand or kiss him goodbye? By the time she'd decided, he'd gone, and it was too late for her to do either. She watched him walk away.

Doing That

'We used to hold hands,' Grandpa whispered. 'We kissed.'

'No!' I said. I was shocked. I wanted to ask him what it was like but I decided against.

'It was...' He paused and shook his head. 'No. I shouldn't really say. I've said too much already.'

I could see that his hands were trembling and his face was pale. Even with the energy levels turned down low and the screen flickering and twitching, he looked nervous, rattled.

'Maybe we should change the subject now,' he said. 'Maybe you ought to tell me about your day instead.'

'OK, Grandpa. That's cool.'

What had my day been like? Much the same as usual. Working on my literature coursework. Reading, downloading, highlighting, annotating, logging, saving, filing, copying, pasting, sometimes trashing. Quite a lot of trashing actually. It wasn't going well. Lunch? A hot cheesy thing, a glass of thick chocolate milk. Oh yes and my morning fish-oil capsule, for a bit more brain power, and my vitamin D tablet, of course, and my sex dampener. No choice. Just take what's given.

'My day's been fine, Grandpa. Same as always. Working on my essay for the Old Lit course.'

I was being careful. I didn't want to say too much. Just like him. Careful.

What I really wanted to say was that after I'd eaten my lunch, my day had taken a surprising turn. I wanted to ask him about it. After all, he'd lived a long time. He knew things I didn't. He might be able to calm the thundering in my ears, the blood that kept rushing to my face, the uncomfortable stirrings. I wanted to say, 'This afternoon, something very strange happened, Grandpa. That's why I asked you about that other thing, the thing I shouldn't have asked you. The thing about you and Grandma that I shouldn't have said. I came across something... '

But I'd clearly already said enough. I couldn't say more.

'I've got to go now, Ben,' Grandpa said. 'There's a couple of people queued up to speak to me online.'

He seemed in a hurry to get away. I wondered why. He was usually keen for a chat. He waved to me and touched his hand to his lips, in a touchingly old-fashioned gesture.

'Bye, Ben, my boy. Call again soon! Oh, and forget that thing I said to you earlier about your grandma and me. It was nothing.'

Then his image on the screen froze, there was the usual lurching whurrup and he was gone.

He'd kissed her. Wow. It was a surprise. A shock. I'd known Grandma Myers before she died and I really couldn't imagine it, Grandpa and her doing that! I'd read about it of course. There'd been a worksheet once at school, with hints of other things too, even more extreme. But it didn't go into detail and that had seemed no bad thing. The kissing idea was quite enough for me to take in.

To think that only fifty or sixty years ago it had been happening regularly, and even Grandpa and Grandma had done it. To be honest it made me feel a little nauseous, dizzy. The table and the chairs seemed to have given up their gravity. They were rippling around the room. I was glad he'd signed off without saying more.

'Calm down,' I said out loud to myself. 'This is just silly.' But it was hard to get that picture out of my head – Granny and him. And what for? That was the most difficult thing to understand. Why? When all the downsides were so obvious.

My parents had never gone in for that kind of thing, I was absolutely sure of that. Mother had always been quite straight with me about personal relationships. She believed in honesty. No point in hiding things and giving a child all kinds of psychological hang-ups. She'd met my father in the usual way and stuck by the rules. They'd admired each other's doctoral theses, liked each other's styles of writing, felt a strong connection in their love of music. They'd had a lovely old-school wedding, bringing all their friends together for a party online, choosing music downloads from their favourite era. I'd watched my parents' wedding a few times on playback. It was sweet. But also, if I'm honest, a little embarrassing, listening to those bands with those out-of-tune plinkety-plonkety guitars and funny old booming drum kits. Fine for a music history course maybe but not much more.

Mother and Father weren't kissers, I was sure of that. No way. And just suppose they'd wanted to be, it'd have been pretty hard to organise. Finding each other and meeting up, just for starters. The penalties, even in those days, would have been harsh. It wouldn't have been worth it.

The kissing thing, like all the rest of what they did way back then, had never really been of great interest to me. You know what they say, what you don't know about you don't miss. And the screen stuff they provide usually does the trick, if I'm ever feeling a bit in need of something, or if the sex dampener hasn't quite kicked in. Though reading those novels for the Old Lit course had somtimes got me wondering. What exactly were those blacked-out bits? Why bother doing all that shading out of the text if it was all so dull and completely valueless? Redaction for redaction's sake didn't make much sense.

That thing – kissing – hadn't seemed very important at the time, though. But now, since lunchtime, it's just about all I can think about.

You see, straight after lunch I went back to my essay. I was doing my usual search on the web, just looking for a few references to add to my footnotes, when I came across this site. It shouldn't have been there. It should have been blocked, or had warnings in place at the very least. I shouldn't have been curious. I shouldn't have opened it. And if I'd opened it, I shouldn't have read it. But I did. I did open it and I did read it.

It was a short story by a Russian. An old one, from way back when. We're not supposed to read his work because it's not significant apparently. That's what the teachers say. This Russian, Anton, from Chekhov or somewhere, took fiction in a bad direction, all the critics agree, so his stories are not on the syllabus. Not worth studying, they say. But there it was, open on my desktop, and there was the title and there was the print, sitting on the screen, in Times New Roman of all the stupid things, just begging me to read it. So, I did. I read it.

'The Kiss'. That's what it was called. A long time ago – even further back than when Grandpa and Grandma Myers were young – when women wore long dresses and men carried guns and fought in real wars, a young man goes to a party and a young woman mistakes him for someone else and kisses him. And then all he can think about is that kiss. His whole life narrows down to that one moment, when her arms are around his neck and she kisses him. He imagines meeting her again and the disappointment, oh the ache of sadness when he goes back and nothing happens. Zilch. All that yearning for her comes to nothing. For a kiss. Just a pointless, germy old kiss.

I read it all, in one sitting, just like that. My face was hot. Did I have a fever or something? I got the thermometer out from the cupboard. It was normal. My pulse was hammering. There was something very odd going on in my head. I didn't feel good. But then I didn't feel bad either. The man in the story by that old writer, from Chekhov or somewhere, had been a complete fool, an idiot. So why did I like him? And why did I want, so very badly, for the young woman, whoever she was, to kiss him again?

Now I'm sitting at my desk in front of the screen and I can't concentrate on my essay and I can't stop thinking about it, about the young man who wanted to kiss the girl again. And about Grandpa and Grandma and all those other people way back then.

I should get on with my work. I'm late with my essay and I'll get penalty marks if it's not in by tomorrow. But I'm looking for that site. I want to read that story again. I want to find out why the kiss was so important, why the young man had to kiss the girl again. But I'm searching for the site and I'm frantically looking at my online history and the screen's twitching and flickering and sparking and I'm trying to remember the search words and when I finally do, all I find is my screen telling me, in big red letters, 'SITE CLOSED INDEFINITELY FOR MAINTENANCE'.

So that's it then. Deleted. Not even redacted. Completely wiped. Gone.

I go back to my essay and swallow my afternoon energy capsule and message my friends and text my mother to say hi and fire off a little help bomb to the engineers to tell them my screen's playing up and I want it fixed.

And then I send a little video greeting to Gramps to say sorry if I made him concerned earlier, with all my questions. And that I'm fine. Honestly. And not to worry about the thing I asked him about, the thing that he and Grandma Myers once did. It was nothing. I've forgotten about it already. It really wasn't important. Honestly, it wasn't important. Not important at all.

Habit

The first time she wore the outfit to go out was on a Saturday night. The manager of the coffee shop where she worked had arranged the rota in her favour so that she had the whole of the Friday and Saturday off – his way of thanking her, perhaps, paying her back. On Friday evening he came round to her flat straight after closing up and stayed for an hour, before going to collect his eldest daughter from her ballet class.

On the Saturday morning, she dressed up in the outfit and ate her breakfast wearing it, not only the veil but also the coat. She didn't bother with the tights and shoes, remaining in her fluffy blue slippers instead. She washed the dishes in her outfit, did the ironing and cleaned the kitchen. At one point she put on Radio 2, then switched it off again. It didn't seem right. In the quiet that followed, she found herself humming gently, a repetitive little tune that seemed to go much better with mopping the kitchen floor in a gabardine coat and veil.

She got the idea from *Ida*, a film she'd seen about a Jewish woman living in Poland after the Second World War who had decided to become a nun. She'd gone to see it with the manager, on an evening when his wife was busy. She wondered what had attracted him to this particular film. The woman's name in the title, perhaps, or the image on the poster? It was a surprising choice. He was restless in the cinema, paying more attention to her than to the screen, stroking her hand, touching her thigh. She, on the other hand, was transfixed. The young woman in the film, a novitiate, had a lovely face that drew you in and filled the screen with light – mesmeric and unfathomable. She left the convent for a time and went into town. Wherever she went, people trusted her. Had they known she was Jewish, their eyes would have narrowed with suspicion but with her novice's headdress on, she was treated with respect. They asked her to bless their children, gave her somewhere to sleep for the night, apologised for any small act of impoliteness, intended or not.

When the film was over, the manager had offered to take her home. Though she would really rather not have done so, she allowed him to come up to her flat where she let him, standing in the front hall, without any preliminaries or niceties, pull down her pants and push himself inside her. He had done it once or twice before and now it was hard to say no. It was over quickly and he left straightaway, not even waiting for a cigarette or a coffee.

After that evening, she took to wearing a nun's veil – not at work, of course, and not every day, just every now and then, when the fancy took her, when she decided she'd had enough of the usual routine of waitressing, the local authority gym, the manager.

She made the veil herself, buying the dark serge material at a haberdashery, looking online for images to guide her in its construction. In the end, she chose something simple that she thought would frame her face rather well. Looking in the mirror, she was satisfied with the result. Her features took on a purity and clarity that were lost when her hair tumbled around her face in its usual unruliness. Seeing herself in the mirror, she already felt different – somehow calmer, more in, or under, control.

She bought a coat for herself at a charity shop, a grey gabardine with a belt, shapeless, slightly longer than it need be but a decent enough fit. If she cinched in the waist tightly it became something else, accentuating her hourglass figure – it had those kinds of possibilities. But for now, she allowed it to hang loose and limp around her body. She found some tan-coloured tights at the back of her underwear drawer and pulled out a pair of flat black pumps – not ideal but they'd have to do.

For a few weeks, all she did was try on the clothes in her room. She experimented with poses, kneeling at the end of her bed, her hands brought together in the shape of prayer, sitting at her table, clasping a book in both hands, crossing herself in front of the mirror. She tried out faces in front of the mirror – humble, faithful, penitent, beatific. Beatific? What was that like? Her life hadn't prepared her for that look. But a small smile appeared to do the trick – eyes looking straight ahead steadily and a light smile playing on the lips.

On the Saturday afternoon, the manager was back for half an hour in between the lunchtime rush and the start of the afternoon shift. She let him take off her top and touch her breasts before pulling down her jeans but she turned her head away when he tried to kiss her.

On the Saturday evening, she was supposed to be going out with Carla, the girl at work who was trained to make the coffee. They'd agreed to go out for a meal and to a club. But Carla called to say that she had decided to stay in instead – she didn't fancy a night out.

Now she had nothing fixed, nothing to do. She put on her nun's veil and her gabardine coat and sat for some time looking at herself in the mirror. Then she took her purse and keys, slipped them into the deep pocket of the coat and went out, shutting the door of her room behind her. She stepped softly down the stairs and out of the main door, into the busy street below.

In the street, she hesitated. Where should she go? There was a church just around the corner but why would she want to go there? All around her was the usual bustle of the High Street – teenagers clustered around the Tube station, shrieking and flapping like noisy geese, sweaty market traders putting half-empty wooden crates into the backs of vans, tattooed young men sloshing cans of beer over both the pavement and themselves, heavy women struggling to balance their own weight between laden carrier bags from the supermarket. A dull-eyed, mangy-looking young woman sat in a doorway, wrapped in a dirty duvet, while a sprightly dog skittered at her feet.

'Sister! Oy, Sister!'

It took her a while to realise that someone was shouting at her.

'A cup of tea for you, if you want it. On the house.'

It was the man from the tea van. She'd had a run-in with him once, when he refused to acknowledge that she'd given him a ten-pound note rather than a fiver.

'Thank you,' she said and took the foam cup from him.

'Blessings on you,' he said.

She muttered something indistinct under her breath and walked away.

The tea was hot and sweet – he'd put two sugars in, at least. And though she usually drank her tea without, it seemed like a sudden luxury, for which she was grateful to him.

At the traffic light she stepped to cross while it was still green, a moment of inattention rather than her usual deliberate hurry. A white car with tinted windows coming speeding towards her screeched to a halt and stopped. As she passed in front of the car, the front window was lowered. A young man leaned out, his arm jutting out of the window, his diamond earring flashing at her.

'Watch out,' he shouted. 'You'll get yourself killed if you're not careful!' Then, as she raised her eyes towards his and held them there in a steady gaze, there was a more flustered, 'Sorry, Miss... Madam! You mind yourself, lady. Take care!'

She nodded silently and before she knew it she had made the sign of the cross at him. He smiled sheepishly and gave her an awkward childlike wave before driving on.

'Bless you,' she thought.

At the bus stop a group of raucous girls went silent as she approached, unable to stop themselves from staring at her. Once she'd passed, she heard one say to the rest, 'She's not that much older than us,' and another said, 'What a shame!' Soon the laughter and loudness of a Saturday night out took over again and she was forgotten.

She wandered the streets for a few hours, then returned home, pulling off her veil as soon as she entered the front door, in case the other tenants might see her and wonder. That night she slept soundly for the first time in many months and awoke feeling refreshed and calm.

Over the next few weeks she started going out like this more often. When Carla suggested getting tickets for a gig or meeting up for a drink, she declined. She was too busy, she said. As time went on, she began to expand her repertoire, adding extra, more interesting routines. Riffling through her jewellery drawer she found a cheap necklace. With a bit of alteration it would make a good set of rosary beads. At the charity shop she found a small prayer book which she bought, along with another Nordic noir thriller to read in her breaks at work. She took to washing her face with water and cheap soap and, on her nights as a nun, she wiped off all her make-up and went out exposed and bare. She even considered abandoning her razor and allowing her armpits and legs to grow thick with hair. This was a temptation that she held out for herself as a possible future pleasure, not one that she was able to give in to now.

At work, everything was as it ever was, shouting coffee orders to Carla, collecting used cups, filling containers with sugar and jugs with milk, taking her turn on the till. She wore her usual short black skirt, her white shirt that was a bit too tight over her breasts and her earrings that jangled when she shook out her thick hair before tying it up again as the rules required. Men still asked for her number and the manager still pressed himself up against her when he thought Carla, Roberto and the new Polish girl weren't looking. But once home, she had a shower and changed into her nun's clothes straightaway and spent the evenings in solitary contemplation. If the manager called and said he was coming round, she quickly changed back into jeans or one of her minidresses, so that by the time he arrived, she was herself again.

One morning the manager caught her on her own in the storeroom. He pressed her up against the shelves stacked high with bags of coffee and filters and kissed her. He said he'd like to stay over that night – his wife and daughters were away unexpectedly visiting relatives. He would switch the rota so that she was no longer on duty for the afternoon and early-evening shift. She could go home early and get herself ready, he said. She could see the nervous excitement in his face, the anticipation. She nodded calmly. When Carla questioned her, she shrugged. 'He lets me have time off but I pay for it in my own way.'

Carla stroked a finger lightly down her arm. 'I thought so,' she said. 'No point in being silly about it. You need the job.'

She nodded.

In the afternoon, she sat at the kitchen table in her jeans and sloppy top, fingering her rosary and leafing through her book of prayers, unable to settle to anything. By early evening, she felt calm though, lost in her own quiet thoughts, the world beyond banished. She roused herself and began to get ready.

When the doorbell rang, she picked up the entry phone and buzzed him up. Opening the door to him, she felt nothing, no anticipation, no pleasure, no regret, no anxiety, no fear. She looked at him, a light smile playing on her lips, her eyes holding steady, fixing his gaze. A beatific stare. What she saw did nothing to dispel her calm – the look of shock on his face, the confusion, the stuttering, the stumbling apology, the sweaty uncertainty, the sudden realisation of who, or what, he was looking at, the hasty backward step towards the stairwell.

Joy.

But then, all at once, he seemed to hesitate. He held his head to one side. And then to the other. He frowned slightly. He laughed a little. He stepped towards her again.

'Sexy,' he said, kissing her full on the lips. 'Really sexy. Pure, innocent, virginal,' he said. 'I like it,' he said. 'I want to see what's hiding underneath that grey coat. I'd like to rip it off, along with that thing you've got on your head.'

He came in and spent the night with her.

The next morning, after he'd left, she took the veil and threw it in the outside bin. She found a large plastic bag and put the gabardine coat and the string of beads and the prayer book inside. The charity shop was still closed. She left the bag outside and walked on towards her work, her high heels clicking as she went, her short skirt snagging on her tights, her earrings jangling as she shook out her hair.

This One

'Blow job twenty, full sex thirty, anal forty.'

I sat down on the bed as usual and pointed to the chair, a small tatty old armchair, covered with a pink throw I'd just bought from Asda. Make the place a bit nicer, I thought. For them, as well as me.

He sat perched on the edge and looked around. He stared at one thing after another – the table with its red-satin cloth, the kettle and pile of mugs, the floor lamp, with its tasselled baby-blue shade (another of my silly little purchases), the sink and the laundry basket, its used towels slung over the edge.

'Well then?' I said. 'Made up your mind?'

'How about kissing?'

'No kissing. I don't kiss.'

He was only a young lad and not very good at hiding his feelings. I could see on his face that he was disappointed. Maybe this was his first time.

'Why not?' he asked.

'I don't kiss punters,' I said.

'Your boyfriend? Do you kiss him?'

'None of your business.'

'Don't you like kissing?'

'None of your business.'

He wasn't a typical punter. Mostly they were older. Dirtier. Get it over with quick as you can, keep your distance; avoid the smell of their scalp and their mouth. Tell yourself that with a condom you're not really being touched. A piece of rubber between you, like a wall, keeping him out. Wash yourself well after it's over. Get rid of the smell of him fast. The stink of his cock and where it's been before you.

But this one was fresh-faced. Looked like he should have a girlfriend. A shy girl with nice clothes, who washed her hair every night.

'Haven't you got a girlfriend?'

He looked me straight in the eye.

'None of your business,' he said.

I laughed. 'You're a clever one, aren't you.' I looked at him hard. 'What are you doing here, a boy like you?'

He was fiddling with his hands in his lap. 'My older brother set it up. Told me I needed to get a bit of experience. Find out what it was all about. Said I was wasting precious time.'

'Older brothers, they don't always know what they're talking about. I reckon you should be somewhere else. You're better than this.'

‘What about you?’

I laughed again. ‘Me, no. I’m not better than this.’

He was sitting back in the chair now, looking at me. Then he turned away.

‘But you’re not here to talk. You’re here for something else,’ I said. I reached into my pocket and got out a condom. ‘Protection. I don’t do anything without protection.’

‘I’ve gone off the idea,’ he said.

Was it what I’d said? Or did he just not have the bottle? Persuaded into it by his big brother and then too frightened to go through with it. Not the first time I’d seen that, and it certainly wouldn’t be the last.

‘I’ll pay you something,’ he said. ‘But I don’t want to do anything. It wouldn’t be right.’

‘I do it every day of the week, babe. It’s no big deal. Everyone gets nervous sometimes.’

‘No,’ he said. ‘It’s not that. I wanted to see what it was like. But now, I realise.’

‘What do you realise, sweetheart?’ What the hell was I doing, talking to him like this? He was a punter, no more, no less. Thirty quid in my pocket and get him out the door fast. If he didn’t want to do anything, all the better. Over more quickly and still I’d make him pay. Time for another trick or two before packing it in for the day.

‘It’s hard to explain.’

‘Give it a go, sweetheart. But make it snappy. I’ve got a living to make, you know.’

‘I thought it’d be different.’

‘Oh yes? And how?’

‘I dunno. I suppose I thought about the pictures in magazines but... ’

‘But what?’

‘But not the person.’

I laughed. In fact, I fell about it was so funny.

‘You wanted sex with a photograph, then?’

He didn’t say anything.

‘I’m not glamorous enough, is that it?’ It’s true, I wasn’t looking that great any more, a bit too much weight around the middle, hair a bit thinner than it used to be, lines starting to appear where I’d rather they didn’t.

‘No. It’s not that. You’re fine. You’re great. It’s just... it’s not what I thought it’d be like. You... ’ He pushed his hand through his hair. ‘You... exist.’

I had to laugh. I did exist. I do. I thought I got it, what he was on about. But all this talk was sending us in the wrong direction. Not part of the job.

‘You shouldn’t talk,’ I said. ‘It spoils things. Makes it too complicated. I’ll just take off my clothes, we’ll do it and then you’ll go away happy, I promise you.’

‘I think I’ll just wait, till I find a girl another way. Ask someone out or something like that.’

He looked a bit glum, as if that might take him some time, though by my reckoning, it’d be sooner than he thought. That baby-face of his would soon mature into something the girls would be after.

‘Good idea,’ I said. ‘Find yourself a nice girl. It’ll happen soon enough. And I’ll tell you what. I like you, and because I like you, I’m not going to charge you. It was just a chat. A nice little chat. You can put that money back in your pocket and just go off and pretend we never met.'

What was I doing? I must be going mad. A full twenty minutes and nothing to show for it. Getting sentimental. Soft.

'Tell your brother it was bloody brilliant. He'll never know.'

He smiles and says thanks and turns towards the door.

But then he comes towards me and takes my face in his hands and kisses me full on the lips. And I feel the smooth wet softness of his inner lip and he smells of yeast and babies' scalps and sandalwood and sweat and there's the lightest touch of his tongue in my mouth and suddenly there's more, and there's a surge in the back of my head and I feel like light switches are being turned on and I want to pull him closer in and breathe in the sweat and the bread-warm smell of his skin.

So I quickly pull away.

'I don't kiss,' I say.

He frowns as if he doesn't understand. But he's at the door now. A smile and a wave and he's gone.

I put the condom back in my pocket. I count the money in my purse. I'll go home now and let the day end like this, I think. But I don't lock up and go straight home. I lie back on the bed. I stay there for just a while longer.

Like a Kiss

I can't write without a reader. It's precisely like a kiss – you can't do it alone.

John Cheever

Every evening, when her father had retired to his study for his brandy and cigar, and her brother, Bertie, had slipped out the front door, hailed a cab and headed off to quarters of London she had never seen in daylight, let alone after dark, when the lamps had been lit and she had undertaken an obligatory hour of embroidery on a set of silk handkerchiefs – a present for her father's birthday – when Elsie had come in with her cup of hot milk, drawn the curtains, stoked the fire, bobbed a curtsy and asked whether that would be all, when Puss had decided that the day was over, yawned sleepily and stretched out in front of the hearth, when the house stilled and quiet descended and she was sure not to be disturbed, Theodora finally put aside her sewing, crossed the room and sat down at the desk in the small alcove opposite the door.

Her father never used this desk. His was the large, leather-covered rhinoceros of a desk that took up the width of his study, with its inkstand, seal stamp and blotter, set up for important paperwork and business tasks. He had a pile of creamy vellum embossed with his name, a small Japanese jar filled with pencils and a tray for letters. The silver stand for his pens was decorated with a large sculpture of a stag that rather dominated the desk, its proud antlers held high and one leg raised as if about to stamp its hoof. She had never liked it, despite its fine quality and undoubted value. As a child, she had thought the stag threatening rather than noble. In recent years her father was rarely to be seen sitting at his desk, but rather took up his familiar position in an armchair by the fire, reading *The Times* or *Spectator*, with a brandy glass and decanter never far from reach.

The desk in the drawing room was hers. Though it had never been designated as such, unofficially it was acknowledged to be so. Compact, functional but elegant enough, with a drawer in which she could place her paper and a little lock just underneath the handle, the surface was bare, save for a simple lamp, a small blotter, an inkpot and a single pen. She kept the key on a chain that she wore round her waist, along with that belonging to the large chest in her bedroom.

Every evening, at about this time, when she was absolutely sure of not being disturbed, unless by Puss rousing herself to pad over and leap up to her lap in hopes of settling there for a while, Theodora opened the desk, took out her paper, uncorked the pot of ink and began to write. There was no hesitation, no elaborate ritual of preparing her pen, no staring at the painting on the wall to catch hold of a half-formed thought, no pause in the pen strokes. She dipped the pen in the ink and wrote, with a furious energy that sent Puss quickly hurrying back to the rug by the fireplace for a bit of peace. Anyone observing her might have wondered whether she were in a rush to catch the last post, or in a state of extreme anxiety, writing to a dear brother about to go to war, or divulging her secret thoughts to a lover awaiting word from her. Her pen scratched its way over the page with a ferocity that put the paper at risk of tearing, and threatened damage to the pen itself. She had, indeed, broken many nibs in her time, and Elsie was quite accustomed to being sent out in the morning to buy replacements.

In the day, her duties occupied her, but they were often simple things that required little attention, such as checking a menu for lunch, or rearranging flowers in a vase, and, aside from the lady visitors who came for tea, or the obligation to talk to her father over lunch, she had time to think, and her thoughts were all her own. The words collected, pooled, formed into little puddles, then ponds, that swelled and filled through the day, so that by the evening she was ready to plunge straight into the deep lake of ideas. What she wrote was merely the transcription of what was already there, just waiting to be recorded before it might be forgotten. The pool, seemingly, never dried up. There was never a drought.

Sometimes, in the middle of the day, the urge to open her desk was almost irresistible, an idea coming to her with such urgency and passionate intensity that she could scarcely prevent herself. It clamoured to be written down, and fought with the other demands of her day: her brother Bertie's complaints about the kippers being dried out when he came down at midday; her father's requests for help in searching out a lost item; the frequent need to instruct the servants on every aspect of the running of the house, however small. Then, sometimes, she felt the tears come, and her father, noticing her distress, would beckon her towards him kindly for a pat on the head.

In the chest in her room, month after month, year after year, the words accumulated. The layers of paper grew thick, sheaves bound in loose bundles, tied with lengths of fine red ribbon. Each evening before settling down for the night, she placed the newest scribblings into the chest. In the morning she closed and locked it before coming downstairs.

Bertie was constantly asking about her writing. He was probing, intrusive, contemptuous. What was it about? Who was it written to? What was it for? Now, as he came down late for breakfast and helped himself to scrambled eggs and kedgeree, she saw his eye catch the fresh pile of untouched paper on the desk that she hadn't had time to lock away.

'Why do you need such a damned quantity of paper and ink?' Bertie asked. Then turning to their father, he took up his usual half-teasing theme. 'Is she writing to someone, Pa? Some dashing young man who's going to arrive one day, sweep her up and carry her away from us?'

Her father looked at her and frowned with concern.

Where could I possibly have met such a man? Theodora reflected wearily. Who might he be? There is no suitor who would make such an offer to me now. It is much too late. I spend all my days here, attending to your needs.

The thought of this sometimes caused her pain. Most of all, now, she regretted the loss of children. The idea of devoted little bodies running up to kiss her, pressed close to her, seeking her help and comfort, gave her a sharp ache. And the grown-up children, confiding in her, sharing their lives with her. That too would have given her untold pleasure. But it was not to be. Thoughts of a lover or husband had tormented her in her early adulthood, the idea of passionate kisses and being enveloped in the warmth of someone's sheltering arms. But those feelings had faded over time. She had witnessed the marriages of her cousins, of some of Bertie's friends and her own, and rarely did she witness the model of marital affection that had caused her so much suffering when, as a young woman, it seemed so decisively to elude her grasp.

'What's it for, all this writing?' Bertie persisted. 'Writing one of those damned women's novels or something of that sort? A disreputable, scandalous nonsense of some kind? Wanting to be a celebrated lady authoress, or another such plan?'

She remained silent. Her father came to her rescue at last.

'No harm being done,' he muttered. 'She carries out her duties for the household admirably. What she does at the end of the day is her own affair.'

'I write for myself,' she said, painfully, slowly, trying to clarify. 'I put my ideas down. It's just for me.'

'Well,' Bertie said, a forkful of kedgeree already in his mouth, 'I don't get it. I don't understand. But if it's just for you, if it doesn't affect Pa and me...'

It *was* just for her. That, surely, shouldn't be denied her, as so much else had been? She had written three novels, and a bundle of poems – close on fifty she thought, by now, though she'd never actually counted. But, in truth, her writing being just for her wasn't her choice. More than the loss of the handsome husband in his frock coat, and of those brown- and copper-haired children sitting around her armchair, the absence of readers for her writing filled her with despair. Once, many years back, she had sent a little sample of her work to a well-known publisher. She'd waited and waited to hear back and when the reply finally came, a cursory note of barely three or four lines, she'd decided never to try again. The editor had made a throwaway remark about ladies who write that had made her blush with mortification and shame.

She'd not had love, she'd not had kisses and, in her writing too, she was destined to be unpartnered. It felt wrong. Writing was like love. It needed reciprocation, writer and reader coming together and meeting one another in an embrace. This coupling might have itself brought forth offspring, the continuation of a long family line, a dynasty. She read her favourite authors, inheriting from them the traits and qualities that she wanted to pass on. Her writings were the children of the love affairs she'd had with books, with other writers. She'd entered into each one with passion; kisses had been shared, and now she wanted to share these with others. She wanted to reach out and embrace them with her words too.

But her writing was locked in the chest, unloved, untouched. And now it was too late. She hadn't told her father yet, and certainly not Bertie, what the doctor in Wimpole Street had told her that week, when she'd finally summoned the courage to make an appointment to see him. It seemed wisest to wait before divulging what he had said. It would be months at the very least, he had implied, not weeks or days. There was time for her to break the news to her father, time for the tears. For now, she would rather that they did not know.

But the chest troubled her, the solid old oak one in her room, not the feeble, fragile, unreliable one that in the not too distant future would falter and give way. One day soon someone, probably either Bertie or her father – she hoped it might be her father – would open the chest and discover what was there. Maybe they would look at the contents together and laugh, or express surprise at the sheer quantity, the effort that had gone into these scribblings. Perhaps they'd remark on the fact that Theodora had hidden depths. What a surprise! Maybe one of them – her father, not Bertie – would take the trouble to riffle through and read the odd section and take pleasure in some little thing that she had said. Probably, though, the conclusion would be that it should all be burned. Elsie would be called to scoop up all the bundles and take them down into the kitchen, where they would be fed one by one into the roaring fire in the range.

I write for myself, she had always told Bertie, when he asked, but that was not strictly true and now she grieved in that certain knowledge. No kisses from a man, none from children, and the kiss that she could offer to others through her writing had been denied her too. Till her death, that would bring her the most pain of all. And when she was no longer there, it would all be gone. There would be nothing left.

Yet, despite that, the next evening and the one after that, and for all the weeks that followed, all the days that remained to her, she found herself hurrying to her desk as she had always done. The passion had not left her. The pool was still full.

Orange Blossom

She sat at the edge of the pool, letting her feet trail through the water. Dead flies, moths and orange-blossom petals floated on the surface, along with something scummy that might have been a mixture of cheap suntan oil and dust from the scrubland just beyond the hotel boundary. She felt the blaze of the sun on her back. Her mother had warned her again and again not to sit out too long. But this was the last day of the holiday and she stayed there, looking at her pale feet drifting in the water, aware of him, the boy, sitting across the pool, reading his paperback under the shade of the one faded blue umbrella. He didn't look up. If he had, she would have caught the movement.

It was mid-afternoon. Her parents were at the beach and her older brother, Martin, was reading in their darkened bungalow room. There had been another row, and her mother had suggested to her father that they go across to the beach and leave the children at the hotel. She knew what that was about, even though they'd said that everything was fine now. They would probably be shouting at each other on the beach, as they had yesterday and the day before. Once again, the Spanish women, sitting in their black swimsuits, surrounded by their picnics and dark-haired children, would be looking surprised. They wouldn't turn away, as English families might. Her mother would be sobbing; the vein in her father's forehead would be livid and swollen, as it usually was when he was angry or upset.

She had been looking forward to this holiday and now it was almost over. It was the first time they'd gone abroad. Dad had found a cheap package to San Juan, a little seaside resort outside Alicante, with just one hotel, a shop and a beachside bar. No one she knew had ever been abroad. None of her friends had been beyond Eastbourne, Brighton or Poole.

'Two weeks in Spain! You're so lucky!'

Even the word 'package' had seemed exciting and modern. Adventurous. The brochure promised transfer from the airport and all-in meals at the small hotel near the beach. There would be seafood and interesting Spanish dishes she couldn't pronounce, like tortilla and paella.

'Say it like yuh,' her mother had said. 'I think that's how it's supposed to be.'

'Franco's still in power,' Martin grumbled. 'It's a fascist dictatorship. We shouldn't go.'

'Don't be so silly,' her father said, without even looking up from his paper. 'All this political nonsense from you is getting very annoying.' Martin had stomped off to his room and slammed the door behind him.

Her father and mother had seemed to enjoy talking about the holiday. They looked at each other and smiled. She'd even caught them once, holding hands and kissing, before her mother saw her and awkwardly pulled away. She couldn't remember seeing them do that before, though she supposed they must have done in the past, when things were better. She wondered what had made everything change.

'It's going to be super, Carol,' her mum had said. 'Just what we need, what with all that's been going on. A really good holiday.'

What had been going on? Carol wasn't quite sure. It was clear that everything wasn't 'fine and dandy'; her father had stopped using that favourite phrase of his months ago and her mother often looked on the edge of tears.

They'd arrived at the hotel at night and it had been a bit of a shock, waking up to see the small size of the pool, the unmade road and dusty scrubland all around. An industrial digger stood abandoned nearby and the single orange tree outside the hotel gate was covered in grime from the digger's recent efforts. Mum said she was disappointed that they had to cross the road to get to the beach. It hadn't been clear on the photograph in the brochure. Dad complained that the rooms were poky and the tiles on the bathroom floor were broken.

But then, after breakfast, they'd all put on their swimsuits and headed down to the beach for a swim in the sea and everything seemed fine again. They unpacked their towels and spread them out on the sand, under the shade of the red-and-yellow beach umbrellas they had borrowed from the hotel. Carol's mother took a large bottle of suntan oil out from the holdall, along with the sun hats and beach shoes they'd bought at the small supermarket across the road. Her father blew up a striped beach ball. He tested a plastic snorkelling kit, adjusting the rubber straps on the goggles to make them fit.

Carol watched as a group of policemen – or were they soldiers? – came swaggering along the beach, in black leather boots and strangely ominous three-cornered hats. They stopped at each family group in turn, asking questions, demanding to see their papers. She was just getting ready to run down to the sea with Martin but their mother pulled them back. 'Stay here till they've gone,' she said. She looked nervous. Dad, usually so sure of himself, looked away, avoiding the men's gaze.

'Guardia Civil,' Martin said.

'Will they stop and speak to us?' Carol asked anxiously. Her father didn't reply but turned to Martin instead and hissed at him, 'If they question us, let me do the talking. You keep that fat trap of yours shut.'

The men were approaching. They came up close, their eyes fixed on Mum and Dad, unsmiling. But they passed by without comment. And then, finally, they turned on their heels and made their way back up the beach to join the black van that sat waiting for them. The engine fired up and they drove away. There was laughter, all of a sudden, from the groups of Spanish sunbathers, towels were re-arranged, food bags were opened, games of bat and ball started up again, sandcastles built up and knocked down.

Carol and Martin dropped their towels and ran down towards the sea.

'Watch out for jelly fish, Carol,' Dad shouted.

As it turned out there weren't any, but a slick of black oil floating on the water left their legs covered in sticky deposits that wouldn't come off.

'No more swimming in the sea, then,' Mum said gloomily.

The first week of the holiday went slowly. Martin wasn't interested in her; he was too busy reading his books. He didn't want to spend time with her. There were a few other English families but the children were younger than her and Martin. Her mother had assured her that there would be lots of chances to meet other teenagers but it hadn't turned out that way.

Then one night a new crowd arrived on the bus from the airport and the next morning little groups appeared for breakfast, looking pale and tired and a little surprised. They stood surveying the small pool, with its single battered umbrella, the forlorn and dusty orange tree, the beach and the road.

She noticed the boy immediately. He looked a little older than her, perhaps fifteen or sixteen. He stood by the pool, a few feet apart from his parents, as if wanting to put some distance between himself and them. He had long curly dark hair and wore a purple tie-dyed T-shirt and patched jeans, with a leather thong around his neck and a matching band on his wrist. His skin was surprisingly brown for someone straight off the plane from Gatwick, and she thought he was the most beautiful-looking boy she had ever seen.

She saw him kneel down, put one hand in the pool to feel the temperature, glance up at his parents, then turn towards the table where she was sitting finishing her breakfast. She looked away, the blush rising to her face, wondering whether he had seen her, hoping he had, hoping he hadn't, hoping he had.

The following day, her parents decided to get a bus into Alicante. Carol hadn't wanted to go. Despite the size of the pool, and the broken tiles, the oil on the beach and the rubble, she would have preferred to stay at the hotel.

'It'll be easier to stay here,' she said. 'Can't we just do that?'

But Dad was determined.

'We've come all this way and I'm damned if I'm not going to see a bit of Spain while we're here. Your mother and I want to go.'

Carol looked over at her mother. She didn't say anything for a while. And then, 'It'll be fine, Car. Let's go. Anyway, I thought you were bored at the hotel. This'll make a change.'

They got up at the crack of dawn to catch the morning bus and stood by the side of the road, waiting for it to appear, as promised by the hotel manager. The sun was just coming up. There was no bus stop, no pavement, no sign, just a trodden-down patch of grass and Coke bottles, flattened cigarette butts and empty packets, indicating that people had stood there before.

'This can't be the right place, Derek,' Mum said.

'Always so bloody negative. Go back to the hotel if you want to.'

'I will do, if you're going to be like that.'

'Go on. I'll take the kids on my own. We'll have a nice time for a change.'

Then, as if from nowhere, people began to appear, clambering over rocks and wasteland, carrying baskets and bags, in shirtsleeves and vests, woolly cardigans, floral dresses, hair oiled, black, wiry grey, or coiled in thick tresses, knotted in heavy buns or loose and wild, with skin toasted brown, rough and dry, like shoe leather, or wrinkled and flaky and old. Carol liked watching the people and smelling the salty sweat, the garlic, the whiff of sun-baked skin.

Still no bus. But amazingly, she saw the boy and his parents, picking their way over the dents and potholes towards the bus stop. They must be going to Alicante as well. She wanted to look at him but, instead, turned away, pretending not to have noticed their arrival.

Her parents nodded towards them and muttered, 'Hello.' Martin stood awkwardly, looking down and scuffing his sandals in the dirt. Why wasn't he more confident? Why couldn't he just casually start to talk to the boy? He was the older one, after all. It would make everything so much easier for her, if only Martin would start chatting and she could join in.

Then finally the battered old grey bus came rattling towards them along the dirt road, already heaving and swaying with people. How on earth would all these others fit in?

The Spaniards hurried towards the opening doors, pressing forward, and the boy and his parents found themselves close to the door, looking somewhat surprised to be at the front of the queue. They were propelled forwards into the bus by the crowd. Carol could see them ahead, swept up in the surge, paying their money and making their way to the back, where there was still just a little room to stand.

Dad had managed to edge himself to the front and was stepping onto the platform next to the driver. 'Get yourselves on,' he shouted behind him. Carol and Martin pushed their way on just as the doors squeezed closed. But Mum was left standing with a small crowd by the side of the road. The bus lurched forwards and off.

'Hey, stop!' Dad shouted. 'Por favor. My wife. Esposa.'

The driver did not seem to have noticed. A grey-haired man standing near the front raised his arms up high, an old woman yelled, a young man came forward to talk to the driver. There was swearing and pointing but the driver looked straight ahead at the road, gripped the wheel firmly and carried on down the hill.

Carol burst into tears. Women's voices were raised in a roar of protest. A man in a vest with strong muscular arms threatened to take the wheel. The driver slammed on the brakes, the doors opened and Dad and Martin pushed their way off the bus, with Carol following behind. A tiny old woman standing right at the front of the bus stroked Carol's cheek as she passed.

'Pobrecita, poor little girl,' she said.

Carol landed on the dirt verge and tried to steady herself. Dad took her arm to stop her from falling. They stood at the side of the road and watched the bus heading off, rolling from side to side like a fat drunk, throwing up clouds of dust in its wake. Carol could see the faces of the passengers, staring at them through the back window, and the dim figures of the boy and his parents, watching them.

The bus was gone. All that was left was the acrid dust, powdering their skin, stinging their eyes. Carol searched for a tissue up the sleeve of her cardigan but couldn't find one. She wiped her nose with the side of her hand.

'Come on,' Dad said. 'That's our bloody trip done with.' He stormed off up the hill, expecting them to follow.

'Why couldn't you get on the bus like the rest of us?' Dad called out as soon as he got within shouting distance of Mum. 'Our day's been ruined.'

Mum didn't reply, just turned and marched back to the hotel, leaving Carol and Martin trailing behind with their father.

'Typical,' Dad said. 'We come to Spain and what do we see? Nothing. Some holiday, this!'

Carol spent the day by the pool trying to read her book but thinking about the boy in Alicante. He'd seen everything. He'd watched her crying and wiping her snotty nose. He'd seen her father shouting at her mother and marching off up the hill.

At dinner, the boy and his family weren't at their table. Afterwards, she wandered out to the gate of the hotel and saw them in the distance, in the fading light, coming along the road, carrying stripy straw baskets and wrapped brown-paper packages, making their way slowly back to the hotel. Dad wandered up and joined her.

'Just look at all the things they've bought to take back home with them,' he said grimly.

Close by, two officers from the Guardia Civil were standing at the edge of the road, talking to a cold-drinks seller. He offered them bottles of Coca-Cola from his icebox, which they took, seemingly without paying. They were laughing loudly, whether at the drinks seller, at her and her father, or at something else, she didn't know.

By the second week of the holiday, Mum had stopped coming down for dinner by the pool. She missed out on seeing the flamenco dancers and the nightly guitar player, singing his Spanish songs. She said she was tired and preferred an early night.

'It's all fine, Carol,' she said. 'Don't worry. You just make sure you enjoy your holiday.'

But it was hard to do so, knowing that Mum was in her room alone, while she and Dad and Martin sat by the pool listening to the music. When Mum and Dad talked at breakfast, or by the pool, it always flared up into something ugly, and then they went off alone to their room or to the beach, or for a long walk down the dirt road in front of the hotel. She wanted to follow them. But she didn't.

The days passed and she didn't talk to the boy. She sat by the side of the pool, pretending not to notice him. She read her paperbacks and her magazines. She went into the water for a swim and came out. She dried herself on her towel and lay on the best of the faded-yellow plastic loungers. She applied suntan oil. She lay in the sun.

In the evenings, sitting with Martin and Dad, listening to the guitar player or watching the flamenco dancers, she waited for the boy and his family to come down and hoped they might sit at a table nearby and that Dad might strike up conversation with his parents. But Dad had chosen a good table near the front and was sticking to it and the boy's parents made their way each evening to a table near the back, where she couldn't even see him without turning around. She noticed how the boy's father steered his wife through the restaurant, with one hand lightly touching the small of her back, and how she, in turn, touched his arm.

One day, the boy didn't appear at the pool for breakfast and his mother and father were absent too.

They've gone, she thought. I'll never see him again. Her day seemed empty, dull.

'I'm bored,' she told her mother. 'I want to go home.'

But then at lunchtime he was there again, making his way to their usual table. He carried a yellow snorkel and a pair of blue flippers. They must have spent the morning at the small cove, a bus ride away, recommended to the guests by the hotel staff.

She'd stopped worrying so much about Mum and Dad, although whenever she thought about it, there was still that nauseous lurch in her stomach. But it was the boy who took up most of her thoughts. The beautiful boy.

And now here she was on her last afternoon, sitting at the edge of the pool, looking down into the water, and there he was, just a short distance away, under his umbrella. If only they weren't going home. If only they weren't going to be getting the crowded bus to the tiny little airport next morning and flying back to Gatwick. If only she had the nerve to stand up, walk over and say hello. Soon it would be too late. Too late for talking to him, or for anything more.

She noticed a little movement from his direction. He was getting up. He was putting his book down. He was taking off his purple tie-dyed T-shirt and his shorts. He walked towards the other side of the pool and stood looking down into the water. He dipped his foot in, letting it splash a little. He stood up again, stepped back from the edge and seemed to be going back towards his umbrella; he'd clearly decided against a swim. But no. Now, he ran towards the pool, and as he dived in a shower and burst of water and sunlight spattered the poolside. And there he was, under the water, dark hair, brown skin, sluicing silently towards her.

He came up a few feet away and wiped his face with his hand, pushing back the wet hair. He pulled himself out, dripping and pearly wet, to sit on the side of the pool.

'Going home tomorrow?' he said.

'Yes.'

'Had a good holiday?'

'Sort of.'

'Terrible pool.'

'Yes.'

'Not much to do.'

'No.'

'Nice food though.'

'Yes. Nice paella.'

'Oh, so that's how you say it.'

'I think so.'

'Fancy a walk along the beach?'

'OK.'

That evening he came to sit at her table. They listened to the singer performing his songs. Last one, as always, *Guantanamera*, and the usual murmur of pleasure from the audience. She imagined the boy kissing her, under the dusty orange blossom in the darkness of the night, on the dirt road.

The singer put his guitar in its case, clipped it shut and went to sit at the bar, where a glass of wine was waiting for him. Martin took the keys and went off to their room. Her father sat there for a bit, gave her a long, hard look and then said he was off to bed.

'Don't be too late,' he said. 'We're up early for the flight home.'

In the bus going back to the airport her parents sat apart, each on their own, her mother staring out of the window, her father looking straight ahead at the seat in front of him. His face was thunderous and dark, like a violent summer storm threatening to break. It made her think of those policemen on the beach in their black boots and hats, their faces full of a menace she also could not understand. She tried not to cry, for her parents, or for the boy, she wasn't sure which. Under the dusty orange blossom, in the darkness of the night, on the dirt road, he had kissed her. She would hold on to that certainty, no matter what.

The Girl with Tortoiseshell Eyes

He sees the muscles of her face go slack, the pallor draining into grey. She is the colour of his paint water, when he cleans his brush, or the blue-white china when it enters the kiln. The reassuring bleeps are now one determined, hostile note. And so, it is over. And so, she is gone.

He is taken aback by the sequence of his emotions. He must call someone, a doctor, one of the nurses, the orderly he can see outside in the corridor, rhythmically mopping the floor. He must get help. They will revive her, plug her into a machine, thump her back into life. He wants to get up and shake her, snap her out of this obstinate foolishness that seems to have consumed her, this refusal to respond. But it has already been decided between them; he will let her go. Her face is free of pain at last. He feels no more dread. Is it as bad as he thought it would be? Yes and no, neither and both. Who shall he phone first, her sisters, Bea and Cora, their friends Mike and Anne? There is nothing in the fridge at their flat. No milk for tea, if people call. He will need to arrange the funeral. He has attended few, organised none, his older brother having taken care of that side of things when his mother and father died. He thinks about the songs she would want him to play, Bob Dylan or Bach, neither or both. When he'd raised the subject, a few weeks ago, she had shaken her head stubbornly; she hadn't wanted him to ask.

In the corridor, someone is making a slurred, drunken moan: 'Nurse, nurse,' then more loudly, 'Nurse, nurse,' again. A kitchen trolley squeaks its way down the lino floor, bringing smells of gravy and cabbage and the clatter of plates and cutlery. A face pokes round the door. It is the staff nurse who has been with them throughout this final phase. She enters quietly, goes to the bed, then looks over towards him to confirm what he already knows, before switching off the machine.

'Shall I leave you together for a short while?' she says.

He nods and tries a weak smile to show his thanks. She has been so very kind to them.

The door closes and there is silence. He remains seated. He notices that his legs are trembling but his hands are still. He wipes his face on his sleeve and sees the trail of mucus, like a slug's slow path across the wool. He wonders when her body will stiffen and go cold. Should he touch her while she is still warm? Should he close her eyes, as convention seems to demand? Brush what is left of her hair? Hold her? Kiss her? Weep? He lifts himself up from his chair as if to do some or all of these things. He sits back down again.

A siren sounds somewhere in the distance. An ambulance arriving perhaps, or leaving. A cloud passes over and a thin strip of sunlight flashes through the closed blinds, across the room and over the end of her bed.

Her face looks untroubled now. It reminds him of the face she used to adopt when they were right in the middle of a row and he was in full, satisfying fury and she suddenly pulled out, leaving him high and dry, saying, 'I'm not doing this any more. I've had enough.' Bland, she could seem, detached and indifferent. He is overwhelmed by anger towards her. She has no right to leave him. For ever, she once said, many years ago, and he believed her, and for the second time she has let him down, for the second time abandoned him, this time for good.

The day they met, he'd watched her wandering towards him through Regent's Park and hadn't been able to believe his luck when she'd sat down on his bench. She was thin and long-legged and a little wild-looking. She smelt of patchouli oil and the mown grass she'd just been lying on. 'I'm Mary,' she said. 'Who are you?' She had a ring of wilting daisies in her hair. 'My God, what a child of the seventies I was,' she'd said years later when they told people the story. 'A hippie. On the way to Woodstock, with flowers in my hair.' They'd repeated the tale so many times over the years that it didn't matter which one of them told it – the story was just the same and he sometimes wondered if they'd both just made it up. A fairy-tale romance that hid the day-to-day ordinariness of what was to come. 'She commented on my Afghan jacket and my bright-green loons. She offered me a roll-up. I hadn't started smoking at that stage, so I refused. She laughed and I noticed the small chip on her front tooth. I liked the way her eyes were speckled brown and grey. Tortoiseshell. I took her to the café for a mug of tea. And that was that. We never looked back.'

Mary, Mary, quite contrary. The girl with tortoiseshell eyes and daisies in her hair.

He sees the flowers on her bedside trolley, freesias in a vase and daffodil bulbs in a plastic pot, about to burst into bloom. They seem defiantly cheerful next to the empty paper pill container, the plastic water jug, beaker and straws. The cupboard door has swung open. Her old furry slippers are perched on top of a pile of clothes and her cardigan flops an empty sleeve out onto the floor.

Mary, Mary.

They had moved in together, marched to ban the bomb, heard the Byrds perform live, lived through the civil rights movement, Vietnam, Enoch Powell's rivers of blood, the sexual revolution. They were the children of the 60s, baby boomers. They'd broken the mould. So how was it possible they could have come to this?

He looks at her now, lying in the bed. Stripped of her own clothing, wearing the regulation pink hospital gown, she looks old. Not the girl he met in the park, or the young woman whose breasts he had once caressed, or even the fifty-year-old woman who had trailed across Europe with him in a camper van, after he'd taken the voluntary package and they'd retired. Nothing like the heartless woman who'd left him for a while, when they were in their thirties, to go off with another man.

The affair. The sodding, bloody affair. Why did that have to return to him now? Memories of hating her when she'd upped and left to live with his best friend Gavin for six months, then sheepishly asked to come back. He is ashamed to be remembering this now, angry with himself and with her. If she hadn't buggered off with Gavin, he'd be able to wipe out all the minor little irritations, the silly rows, the sniping conversations that were part and parcel of every relationship, and just remember the good times, the great times. He could never completely forgive her for Gavin, even though that was now water under a very old bridge. He wishes he could finally, at the very least, forget, now of all times, if not for always. All he can do is say the usual words, tell himself what he always has, to calm the boiling brew inside. 'Don't be stupid. Count your blessings. She came back. Six months, that was all, then she rang to say she was coming home, if you'd have her. You weren't stupid then. You took her back.'

There is a knock at the door. The nurse looks in. She comes over and bends down towards him and puts her arm around his shoulder. She smells of antiseptic hand gel and hospital food and her own comforting female scent of sweat and skin.

'I'm so sorry, Mr Richards... Dennis,' she says. 'Shall I leave you a while longer?'

He nods. Just a moment longer – him and Mary alone. Together. He pulls himself up out of his chair, goes over to the bed and carefully touches her hand. It is still warm. He feels the dry skin on her knuckles, the slender childlike fingers; he traces his own fingers over the hard, pale crescents of her nails, the tiny knobbly wart at the base of her thumb. He touches the plain gold ring.

He leans towards her, to give her one final kiss, but suddenly feels awkward, shy, as if he's coming close to a stranger, rudely invading a private space.

The time has come. He will not stroke her hair or kiss her face – he is too afraid to say so final a goodbye. But very gently, and as if greeting someone beautiful, the most perfect of women, for the very first time, he bends down, lifts her hand and brings it to his lips.

Acknowledgements

Thank you to all those who have read and commented on these stories, and in particular my fellow writers on the Birkbeck MA Creative Writing course 2009-10, my wonderful colleague Lucy Webster, Blue Door Press authors Annabel Chown, Francis Gilbert, Pamela Johnson and Jane Kirwan, and Jill Foulston who offered excellent editorial advice.

Thank you to Sue Tyley for copy-editing the collection, to Lucy Webster for typesetting and preparing it for publication and to Alex Kirby for the stunning cover design.

Thank you, as always, to my husband Adam Sharples and our children, Gemma and Joel, without whose support this book would neither have been written nor published. And to my grandson, Max, who simply gives me more joy every day that passes.

Finally, thank you to all the short-fiction writers whose work I have read over the years. I offer my efforts as part of the loving embrace that has brought readers and writers together for as long as stories have been told and books have been written.

Printed in Great Britain
by Amazon

50271390R00071